PLAYBOOK

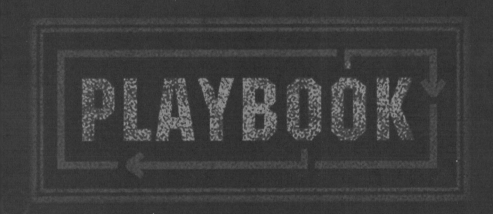

WRITTEN BY
Carl Bowen

COVER AND INTERIOR ILLUSTRATED BY
Eduardo Garcia

COVER COLORS BY
Overdrive Studio at Space Goat Productions

INTERIOR COLORS BY
Komikaki Studio
Featuring SAW33 at Space Goat Productions

LETTERING BY
Jaymes Reed

Sports Illustrated Kids Graphic Novels are published by Stone
Arch Books,
A Capstone Imprint
1710 Roe Crest Drive
North Mankato, Minnesota 56003
www.capstonepub.com

Text © 2015
Illustrations © 2015 Stone Arch Books

All rights reserved. No part of this publication may be
reproduced in whole or in part, or stored in a retrieval system, or
transmitted in any form or by any means, electronic, mechanical,
photocopying, recording, or otherwise, without written
permission of the publisher.

Library of Congress Cataloging-in-Publication Data is available
on the Library of Congress website.

Ashley C. Andersen Zantop PUBLISHER
Michael Dahl EDITORIAL DIRECTOR
Sean Tulien EDITOR
Heather Kindseth CREATIVE DIRECTOR
Brann Garvey ART DIRECTOR
Hilary Wacholz DESIGNER

ISBN: 978-1-4342-6489-3 (library binding)
ISBN: 978-1-4342-9183-7 (paperback)

Summary: Steve's team is absolutely awesome in practice.
Everyone's talented and determined, and their new quarterback,
Aaron Corbin, throws bullets . . . so why are the they struggling
to win games? Steve notices that Aaron seems to be afraid of
getting hit. With a little help from his teammates, Steve goes
to great lengths to toughen up Aaron only to discover that
toughness isn't the quarterback's actual problem . . .

Sports Illustrated KIDS

PRESENTS

QUARTERBACK RUSH

STONE ARCH BOOKS
A Capstone Imprint

CHARACTERS

STEVE MICHAELS

HEIGHT: 5 feet, 1 inch

FEARS: shopping and wrestling

FAVORITE BOOKS: Jake Maddox sports novels

WEIGHT: 108 pounds

SKILLS: (overactive) imagination and problem solving

AARON CORBIN

HEIGHT: 5 feet, 3 inches

FEAR: failure

FAVORITE BOOKS: the Zinc Alloy series

WEIGHT: 135 pounds

SKILLS: passing, rushing, and playcalling

VIVIAN WEISS

HEIGHT: 4 feet, 9 inches

FEAR: losing

FAVORITE BOOK: Jellaby

WEIGHT: 85 pounds

SKILLS: wrestling, loyalty, and toughness

NED KIA

HEIGHT: 5 feet, 8 inches

FEARS: conflict and birds

FAVORITE BOOKS: DC Super Heroes Comic Chapter Books

WEIGHT: 163 pounds

SKILLS: blocking and conflict resolution

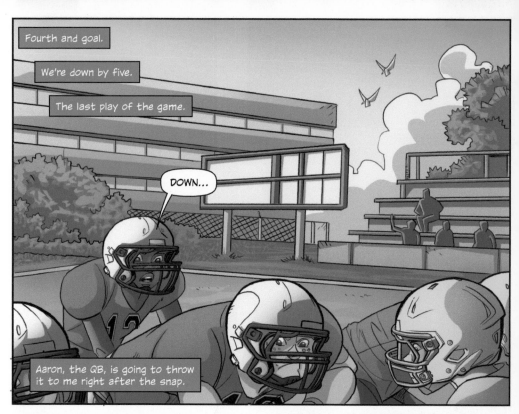

Fourth and goal.

We're down by five.

The last play of the game.

DOWN...

Aaron, the QB, is going to throw it to me right after the snap.

SET...

All I have to do is catch it and run three yards to win the game.

Nine feet doesn't sound like much...

HIKE!!!

...unless you're facing the Wolves, and have an overactive imagination.

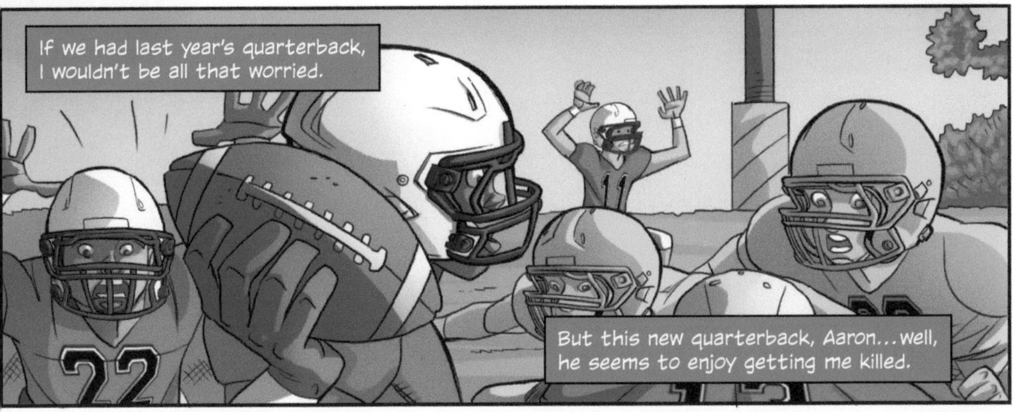
If we had last year's quarterback, I wouldn't be all that worried.
But this new quarterback, Aaron...well, he seems to enjoy getting me killed.

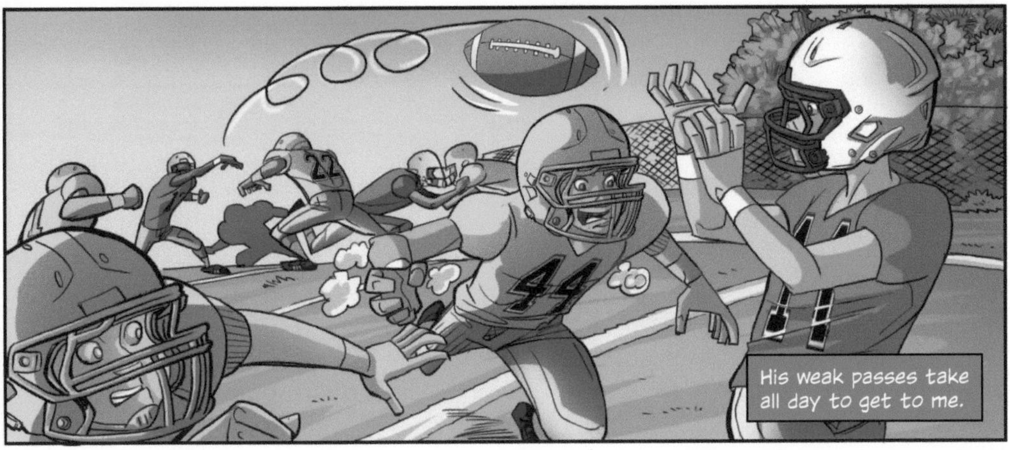
His weak passes take all day to get to me.

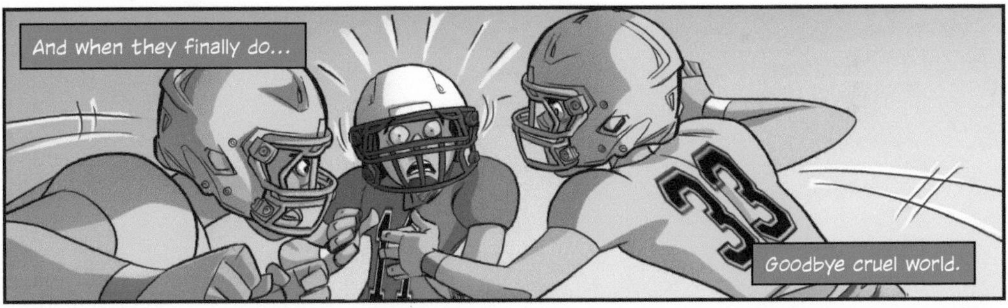
And when they finally do...
Goodbye cruel world.

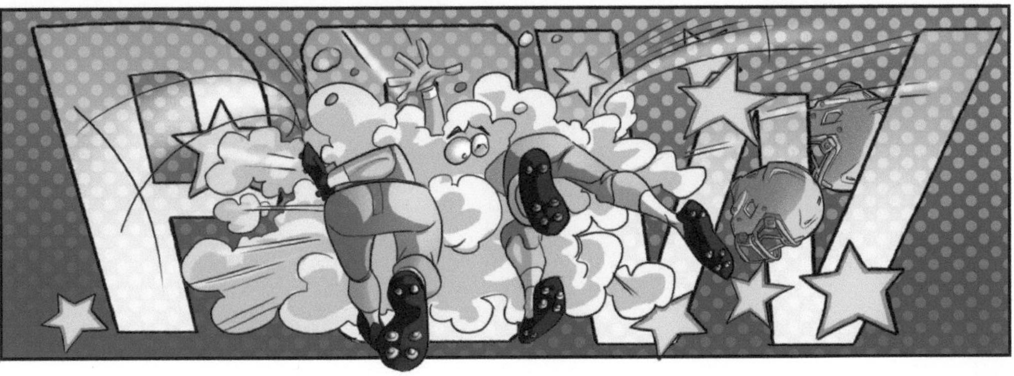

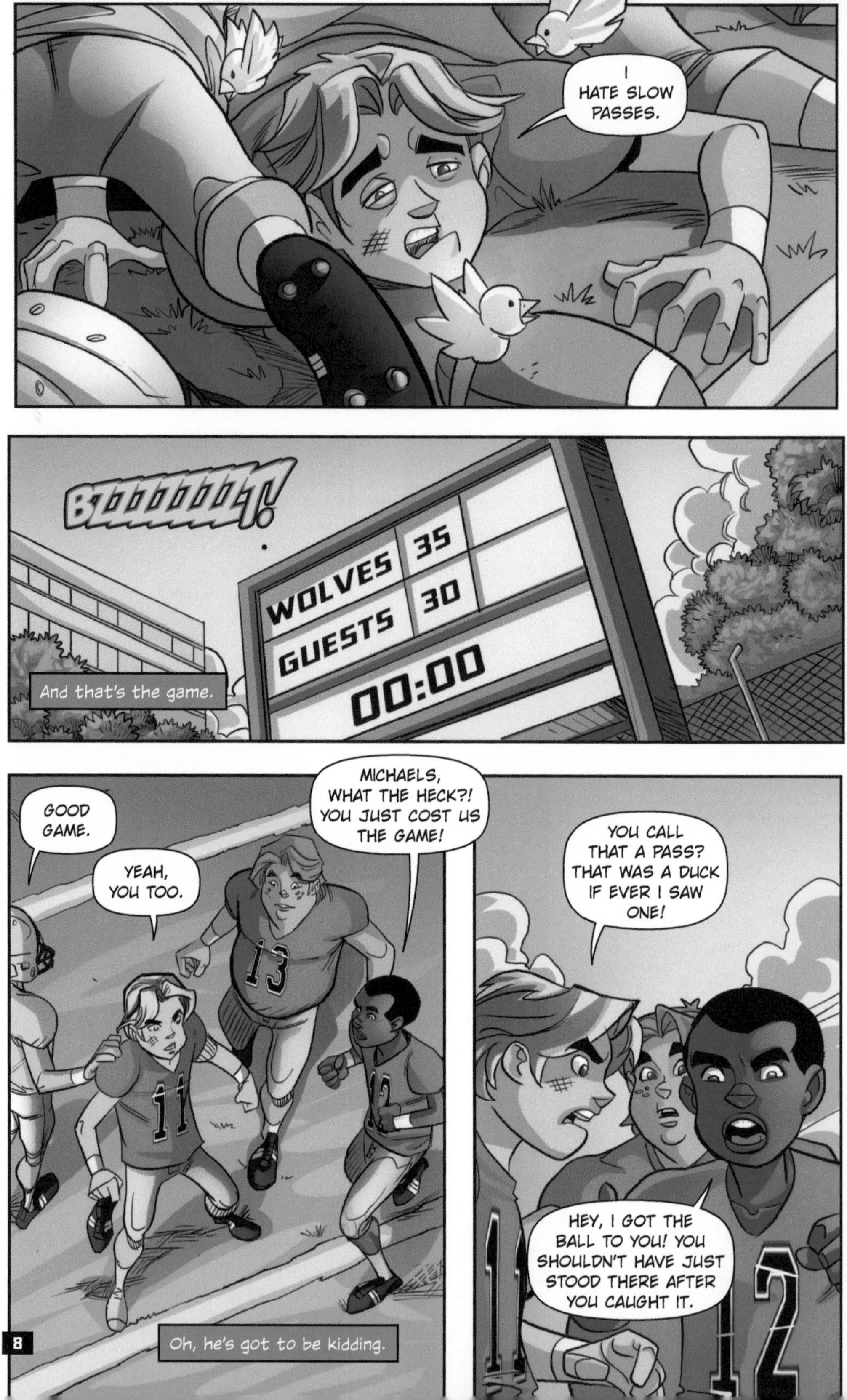
I HATE SLOW PASSES.
BZZZZZZZT!
WOLVES 35
GUESTS 30
00:00
And that's the game.
GOOD GAME.
YEAH, YOU TOO.
MICHAELS, WHAT THE HECK?! YOU JUST COST US THE GAME!
Oh, he's got to be kidding.
YOU CALL THAT A PASS? THAT WAS A DUCK IF EVER I SAW ONE!
HEY, I GOT THE BALL TO YOU! YOU SHOULDN'T HAVE JUST STOOD THERE AFTER YOU CAUGHT IT.

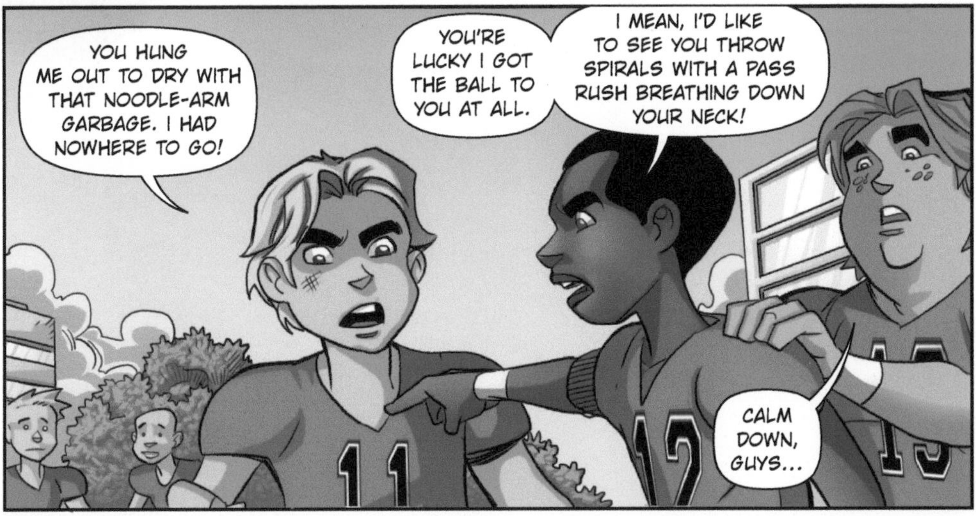
YOU HUNG ME OUT TO DRY WITH THAT NOODLE-ARM GARBAGE. I HAD NOWHERE TO GO!
YOU'RE LUCKY I GOT THE BALL TO YOU AT ALL.
I MEAN, I'D LIKE TO SEE YOU THROW SPIRALS WITH A PASS RUSH BREATHING DOWN YOUR NECK!
CALM DOWN, GUYS...

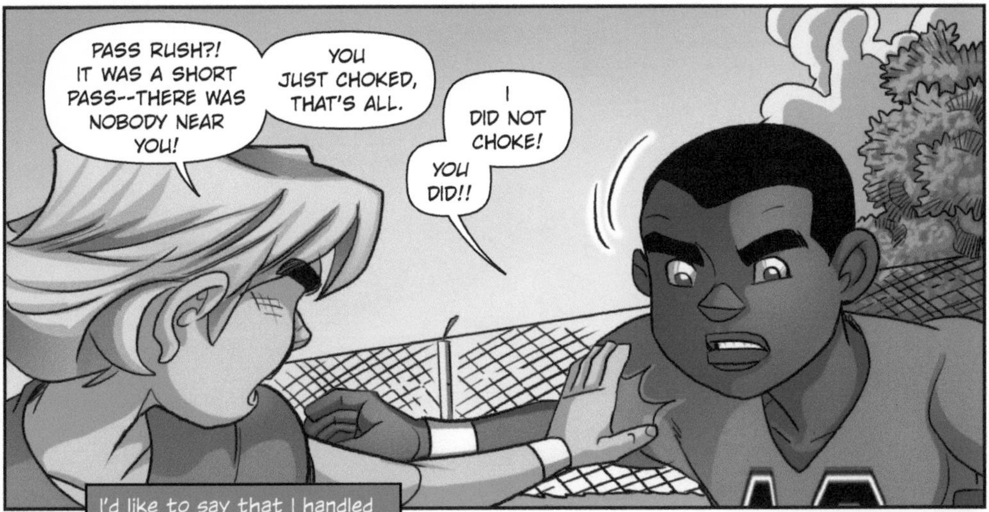
PASS RUSH?! IT WAS A SHORT PASS--THERE WAS NOBODY NEAR YOU!
YOU JUST CHOKED, THAT'S ALL.
I DID NOT CHOKE!
YOU DID!!

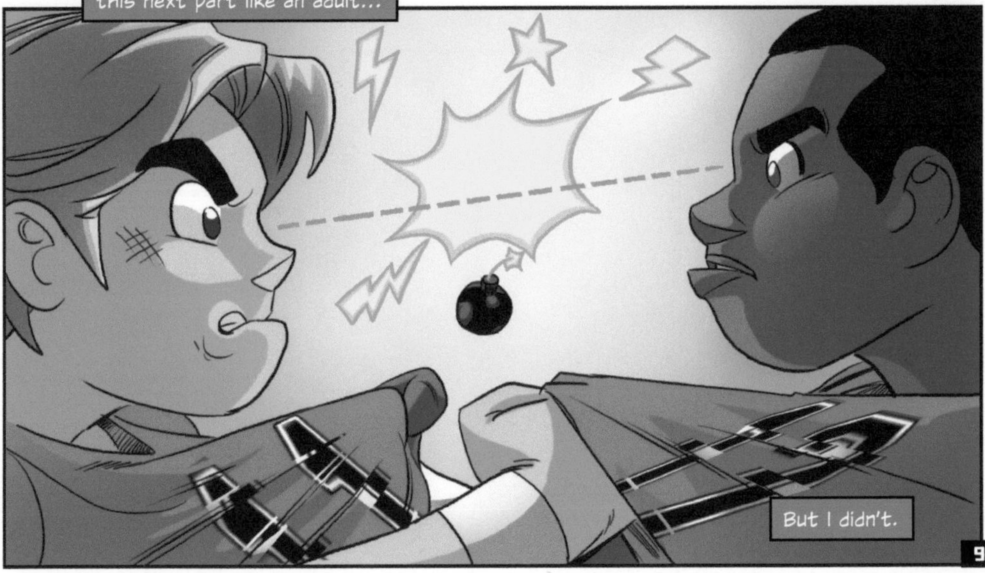
I'd like to say that I handled this next part like an adult...
But I didn't.

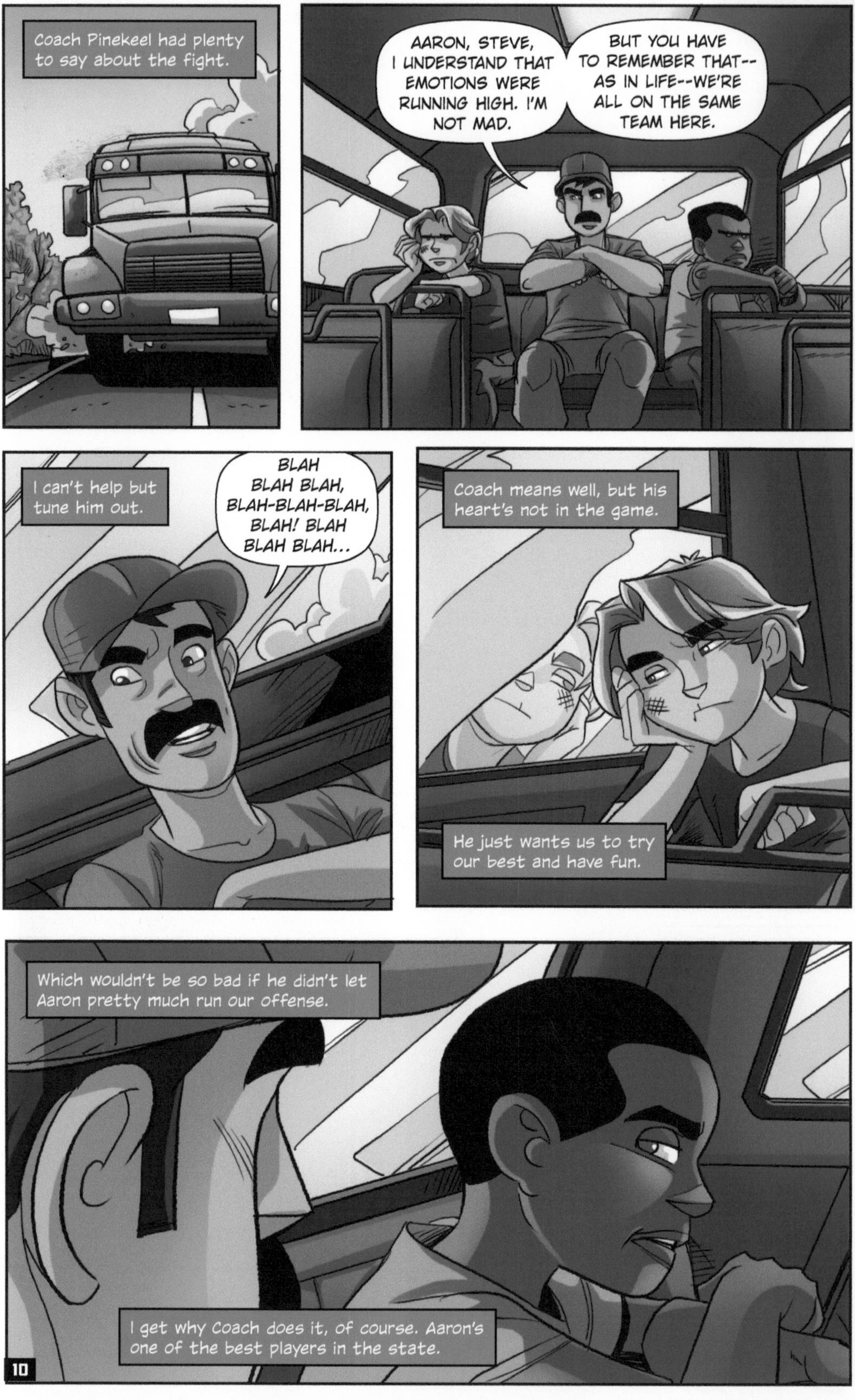
Coach Pinekeel had plenty to say about the fight.
AARON, STEVE, I UNDERSTAND THAT EMOTIONS WERE RUNNING HIGH. I'M NOT MAD.
BUT YOU HAVE TO REMEMBER THAT-- AS IN LIFE--WE'RE ALL ON THE SAME TEAM HERE.
I can't help but tune him out.
BLAH BLAH BLAH, BLAH-BLAH-BLAH, BLAH! BLAH BLAH BLAH...
Coach means well, but his heart's not in the game.
He just wants us to try our best and have fun.
Which wouldn't be so bad if he didn't let Aaron pretty much run our offense.
I get why Coach does it, of course. Aaron's one of the best players in the state.

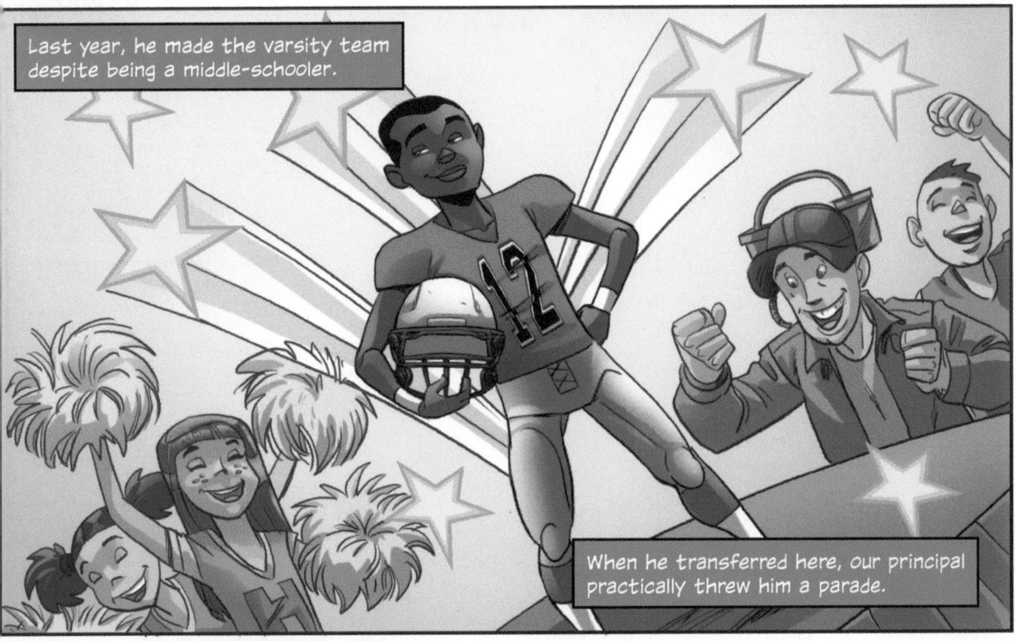
Last year, he made the varsity team despite being a middle-schooler.
When he transferred here, our principal practically threw him a parade.

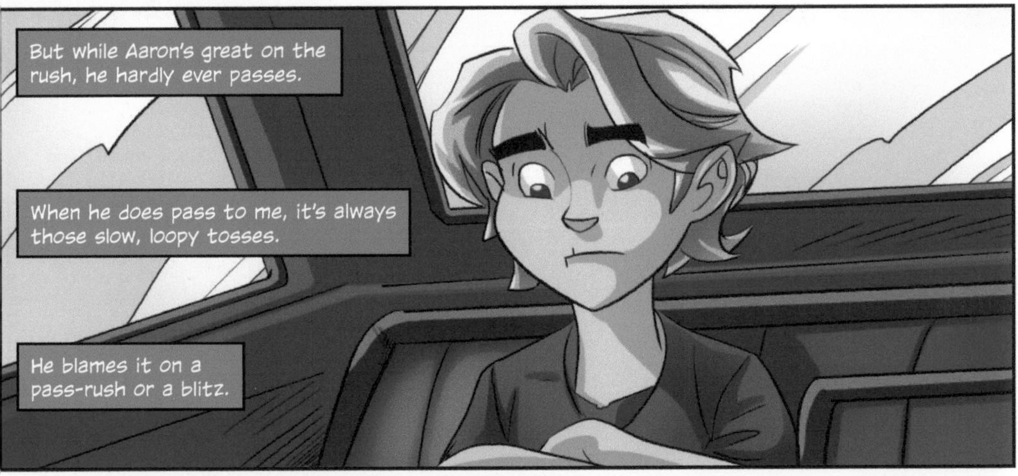
But while Aaron's great on the rush, he hardly ever passes.
When he does pass to me, it's always those slow, loopy tosses.
He blames it on a pass-rush or a blitz.

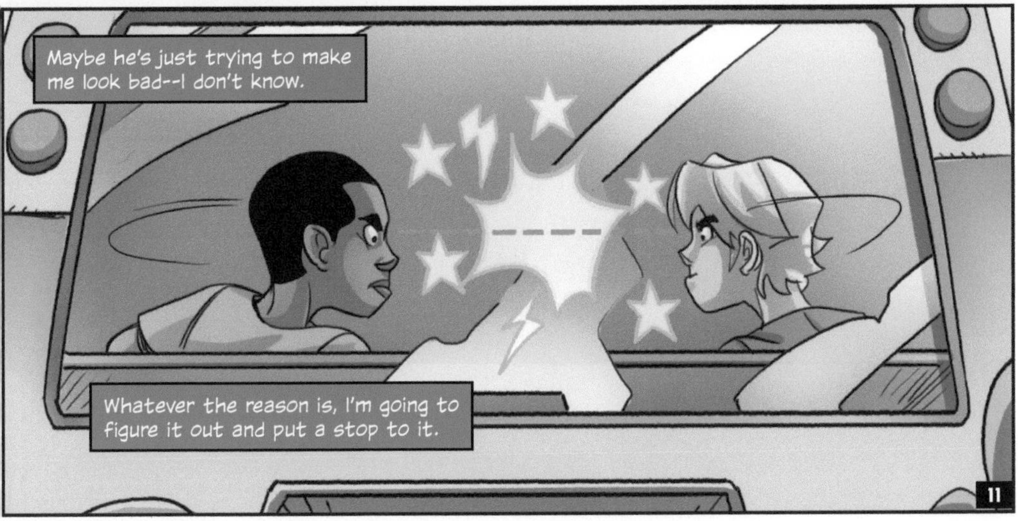
Maybe he's just trying to make me look bad--I don't know.
Whatever the reason is, I'm going to figure it out and put a stop to it.

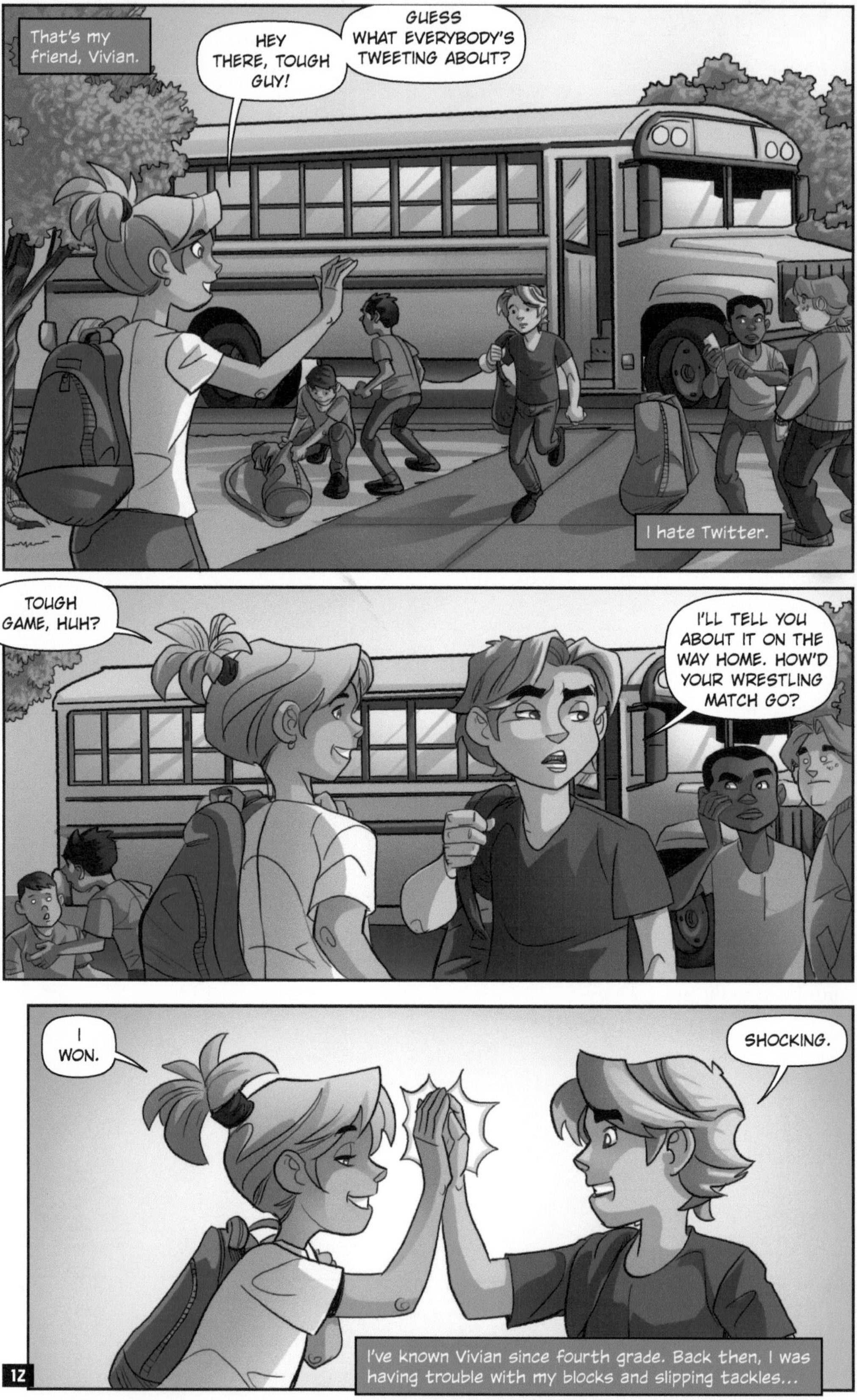
That's my friend, Vivian.
HEY THERE, TOUGH GUY!
GUESS WHAT EVERYBODY'S TWEETING ABOUT?
I hate Twitter.
TOUGH GAME, HUH?
I'LL TELL YOU ABOUT IT ON THE WAY HOME. HOW'D YOUR WRESTLING MATCH GO?
I WON.
SHOCKING.
I've known Vivian since fourth grade. Back then, I was having trouble with my blocks and slipping tackles...

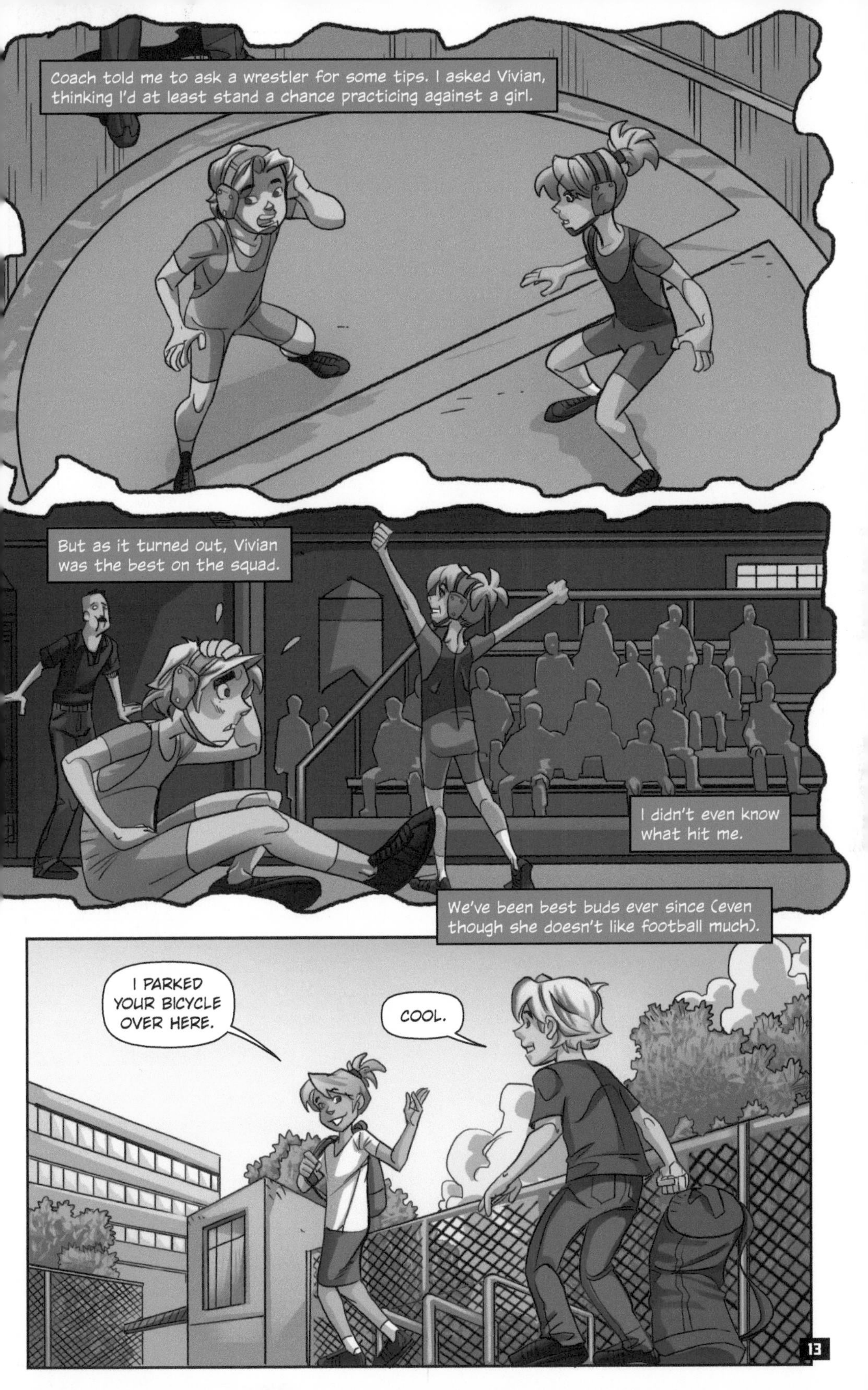
Coach told me to ask a wrestler for some tips. I asked Vivian, thinking I'd at least stand a chance practicing against a girl.
But as it turned out, Vivian was the best on the squad.
I didn't even know what hit me.
We've been best buds ever since (even though she doesn't like football much).
I PARKED YOUR BICYCLE OVER HERE.
COOL.

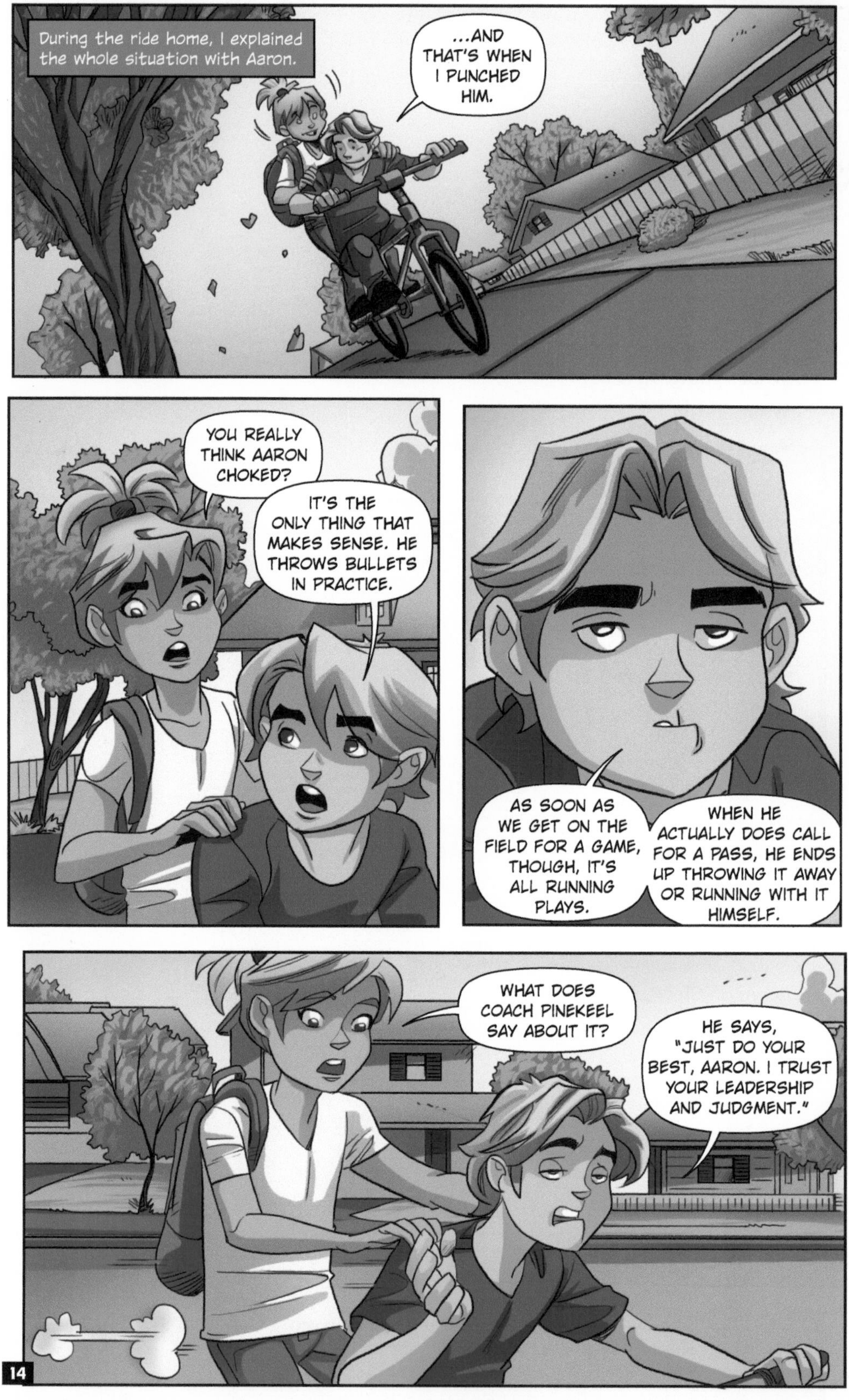
During the ride home, I explained the whole situation with Aaron.
...AND THAT'S WHEN I PUNCHED HIM.
YOU REALLY THINK AARON CHOKED?
IT'S THE ONLY THING THAT MAKES SENSE. HE THROWS BULLETS IN PRACTICE.
AS SOON AS WE GET ON THE FIELD FOR A GAME, THOUGH, IT'S ALL RUNNING PLAYS.
WHEN HE ACTUALLY DOES CALL FOR A PASS, HE ENDS UP THROWING IT AWAY OR RUNNING WITH IT HIMSELF.
WHAT DOES COACH PINEKEEL SAY ABOUT IT?
HE SAYS, "JUST DO YOUR BEST, AARON. I TRUST YOUR LEADERSHIP AND JUDGMENT."

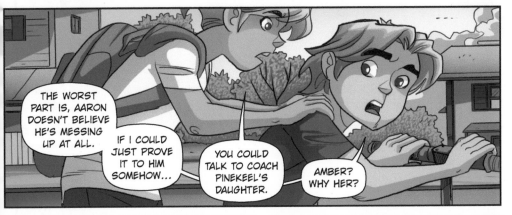

THE WORST PART IS, AARON DOESN'T BELIEVE HE'S MESSING UP AT ALL.

IF I COULD JUST PROVE IT TO HIM SOMEHOW...

YOU COULD TALK TO COACH PINEKEEL'S DAUGHTER.

AMBER? WHY HER?

SHE FILMS YOUR FOOTBALL GAMES FOR THE SCHOOL'S YOUTUBE CHANNEL.

YOU COULD ASK HER TO LET YOU REVIEW THE TAPES. YOU KNOW, SO YOU HAVE SOME EVIDENCE TO SHOW AARON.

THAT'S A GREAT IDEA, VIV! I'LL DO IT TOMORROW.

I THOUGHT WE WERE GONNA GO SHOPPING TOGETHER TOMORROW.

OH, YEAH. RIGHT. THAT SOUNDS...

BORING

...FUN.

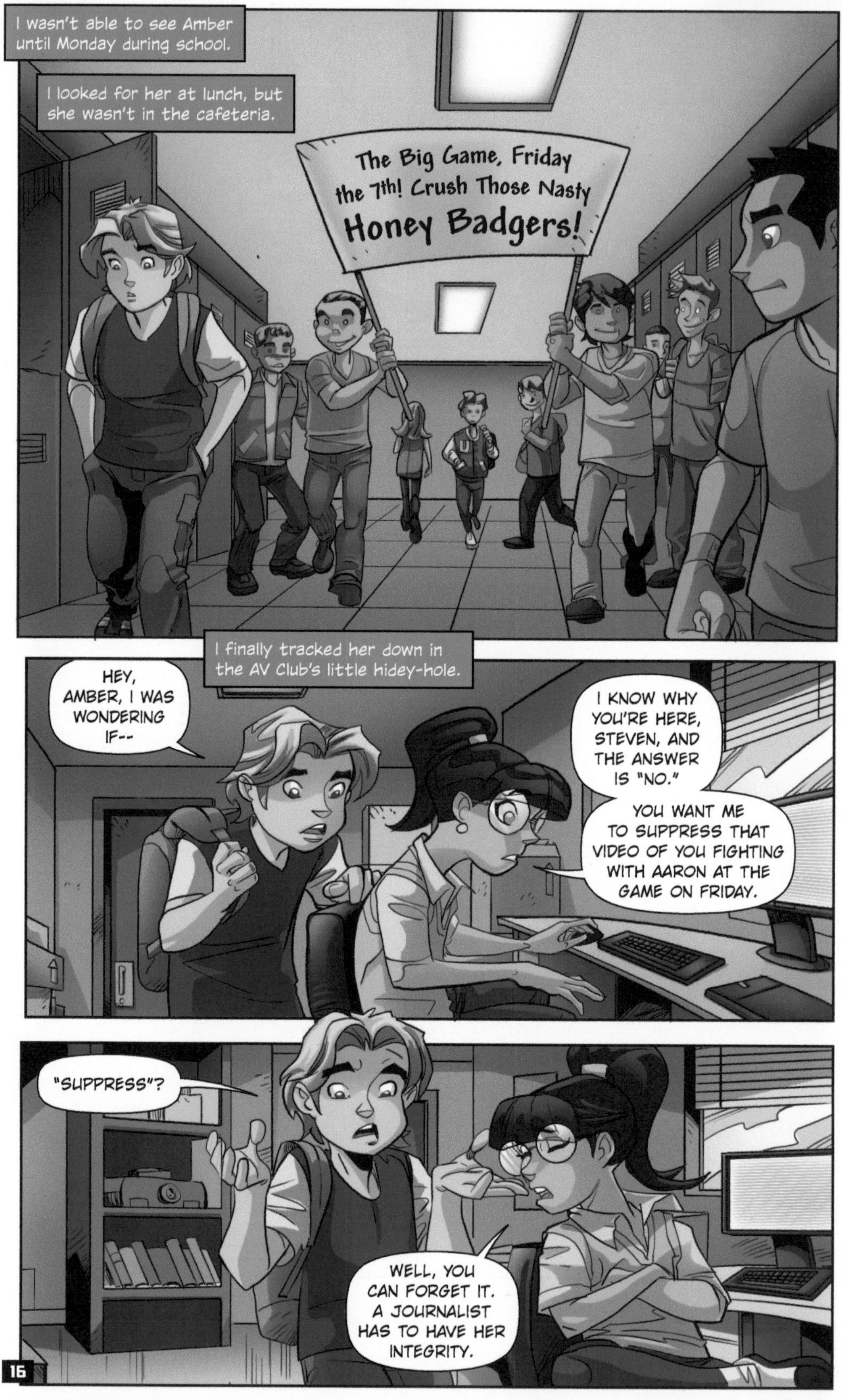
I wasn't able to see Amber until Monday during school.
I looked for her at lunch, but she wasn't in the cafeteria.
The Big Game, Friday the 7th! Crush Those Nasty Honey Badgers!
I finally tracked her down in the AV Club's little hidey-hole.
HEY, AMBER, I WAS WONDERING IF--
I KNOW WHY YOU'RE HERE, STEVEN, AND THE ANSWER IS "NO."
YOU WANT ME TO SUPPRESS THAT VIDEO OF YOU FIGHTING WITH AARON AT THE GAME ON FRIDAY.
"SUPPRESS"?
WELL, YOU CAN FORGET IT. A JOURNALIST HAS TO HAVE HER INTEGRITY.

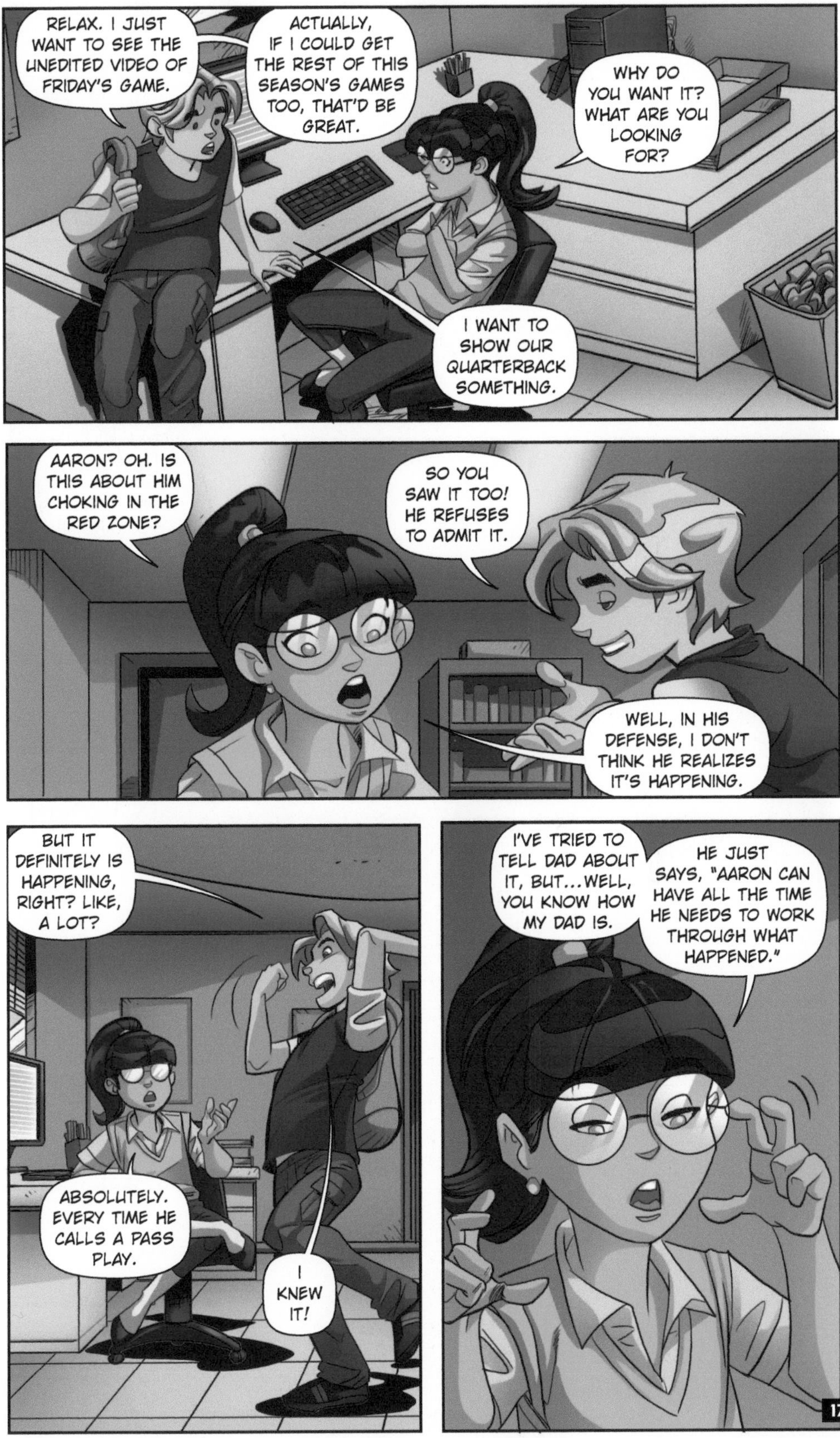
RELAX. I JUST WANT TO SEE THE UNEDITED VIDEO OF FRIDAY'S GAME.
ACTUALLY, IF I COULD GET THE REST OF THIS SEASON'S GAMES TOO, THAT'D BE GREAT.
WHY DO YOU WANT IT? WHAT ARE YOU LOOKING FOR?
I WANT TO SHOW OUR QUARTERBACK SOMETHING.
AARON? OH. IS THIS ABOUT HIM CHOKING IN THE RED ZONE?
SO YOU SAW IT TOO! HE REFUSES TO ADMIT IT.
WELL, IN HIS DEFENSE, I DON'T THINK HE REALIZES IT'S HAPPENING.
BUT IT DEFINITELY IS HAPPENING, RIGHT? LIKE, A LOT?
ABSOLUTELY. EVERY TIME HE CALLS A PASS PLAY.
I KNEW IT!
I'VE TRIED TO TELL DAD ABOUT IT, BUT...WELL, YOU KNOW HOW MY DAD IS.
HE JUST SAYS, "AARON CAN HAVE ALL THE TIME HE NEEDS TO WORK THROUGH WHAT HAPPENED."

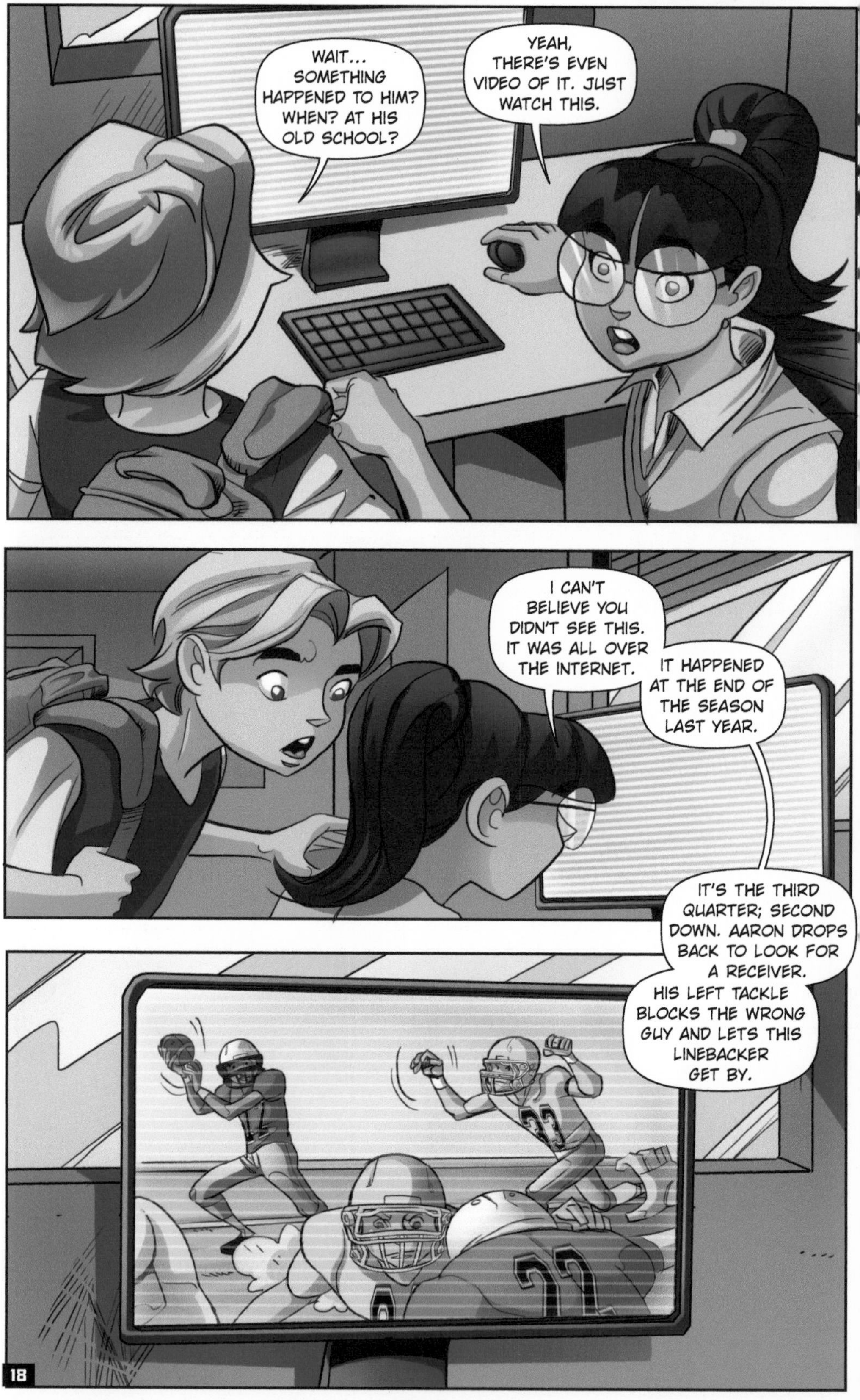
WAIT... SOMETHING HAPPENED TO HIM? WHEN? AT HIS OLD SCHOOL?
YEAH, THERE'S EVEN VIDEO OF IT. JUST WATCH THIS.
I CAN'T BELIEVE YOU DIDN'T SEE THIS. IT WAS ALL OVER THE INTERNET.
IT HAPPENED AT THE END OF THE SEASON LAST YEAR.
IT'S THE THIRD QUARTER; SECOND DOWN. AARON DROPS BACK TO LOOK FOR A RECEIVER.
HIS LEFT TACKLE BLOCKS THE WRONG GUY AND LETS THIS LINEBACKER GET BY.

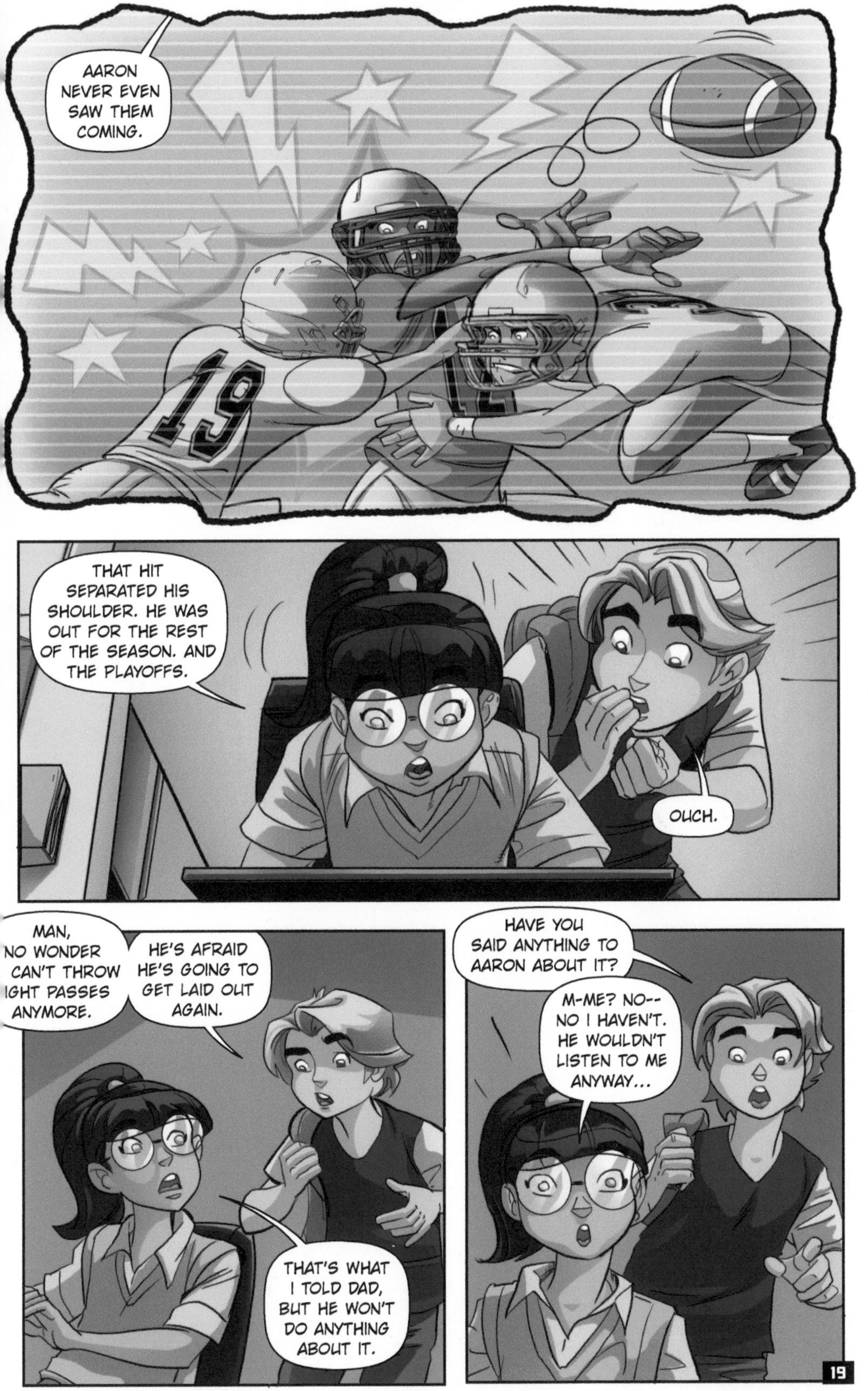
AARON NEVER EVEN SAW THEM COMING.
THAT HIT SEPARATED HIS SHOULDER. HE WAS OUT FOR THE REST OF THE SEASON. AND THE PLAYOFFS.
OUCH.
MAN, NO WONDER CAN'T THROW IGHT PASSES ANYMORE.
HE'S AFRAID HE'S GOING TO GET LAID OUT AGAIN.
THAT'S WHAT I TOLD DAD, BUT HE WON'T DO ANYTHING ABOUT IT.
HAVE YOU SAID ANYTHING TO AARON ABOUT IT?
M-ME? NO-- NO I HAVEN'T. HE WOULDN'T LISTEN TO ME ANYWAY...

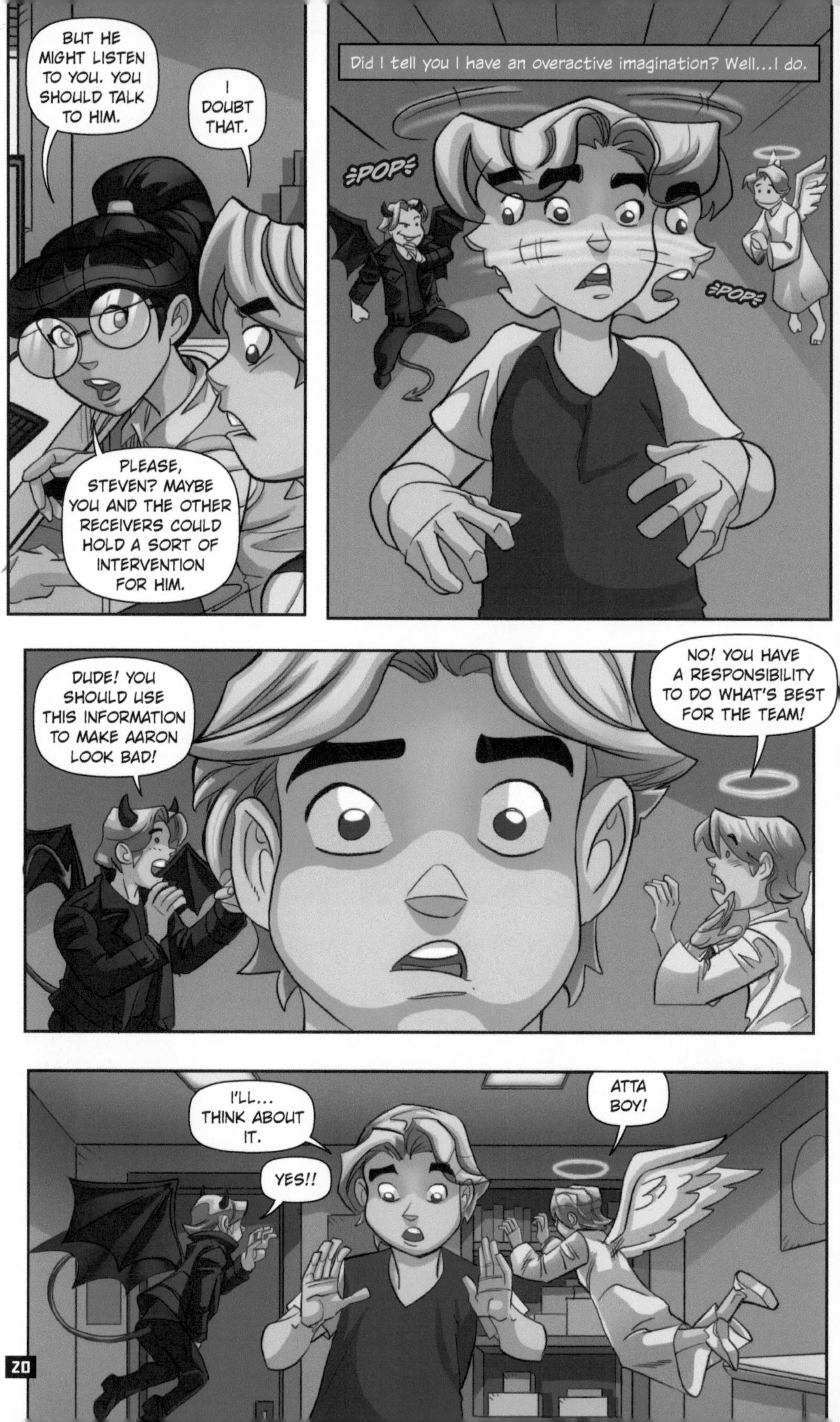
BUT HE MIGHT LISTEN TO YOU. YOU SHOULD TALK TO HIM.
I DOUBT THAT.
PLEASE, STEVEN? MAYBE YOU AND THE OTHER RECEIVERS COULD HOLD A SORT OF INTERVENTION FOR HIM.
Did I tell you I have an overactive imagination? Well...I do.
POP
POP
DUDE! YOU SHOULD USE THIS INFORMATION TO MAKE AARON LOOK BAD!
NO! YOU HAVE A RESPONSIBILITY TO DO WHAT'S BEST FOR THE TEAM!
I'LL... THINK ABOUT IT.
ATTA BOY!
YES!!

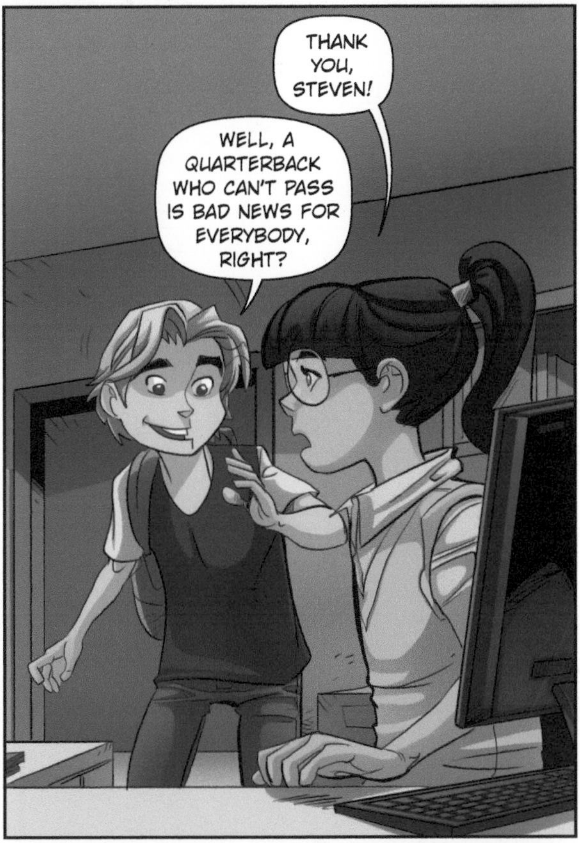
WELL, A QUARTERBACK WHO CAN'T PASS IS BAD NEWS FOR EVERYBODY, RIGHT?
THANK YOU, STEVEN!

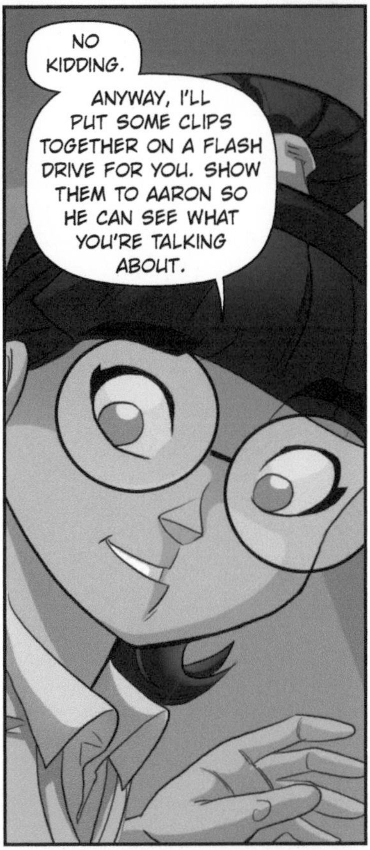
NO KIDDING.
ANYWAY, I'LL PUT SOME CLIPS TOGETHER ON A FLASH DRIVE FOR YOU. SHOW THEM TO AARON SO HE CAN SEE WHAT YOU'RE TALKING ABOUT.

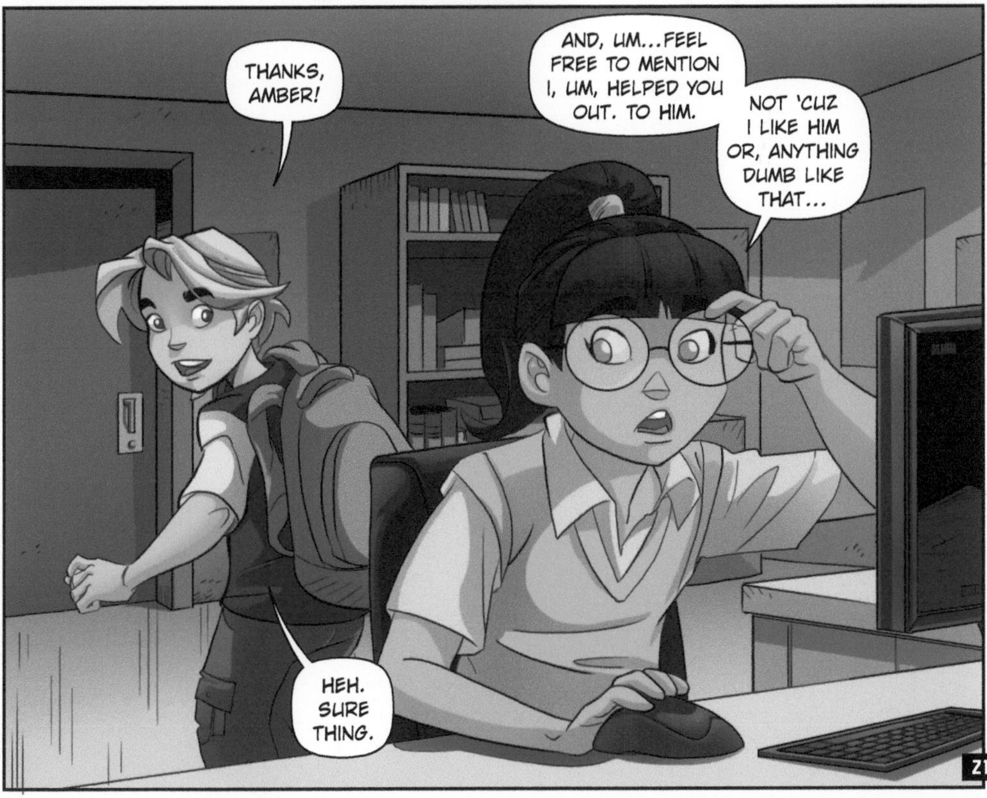
THANKS, AMBER!
AND, UM...FEEL FREE TO MENTION I, UM, HELPED YOU OUT. TO HIM.
NOT 'CUZ I LIKE HIM OR, ANYTHING DUMB LIKE THAT...
HEH. SURE THING.

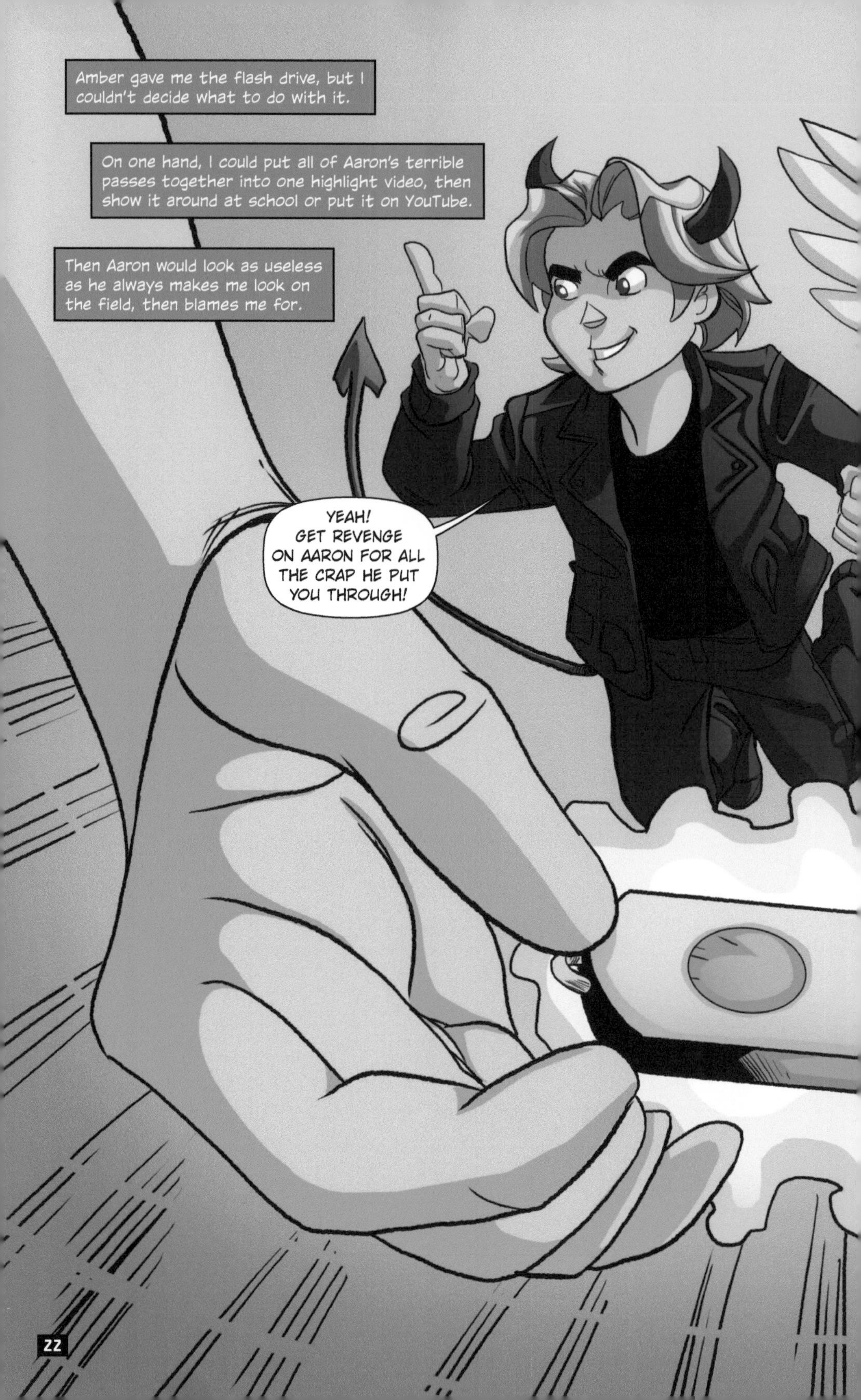
Amber gave me the flash drive, but I couldn't decide what to do with it.
On one hand, I could put all of Aaron's terrible passes together into one highlight video, then show it around at school or put it on YouTube.
Then Aaron would look as useless as he always makes me look on the field, then blames me for.
YEAH! GET REVENGE ON AARON FOR ALL THE CRAP HE PUT YOU THROUGH!

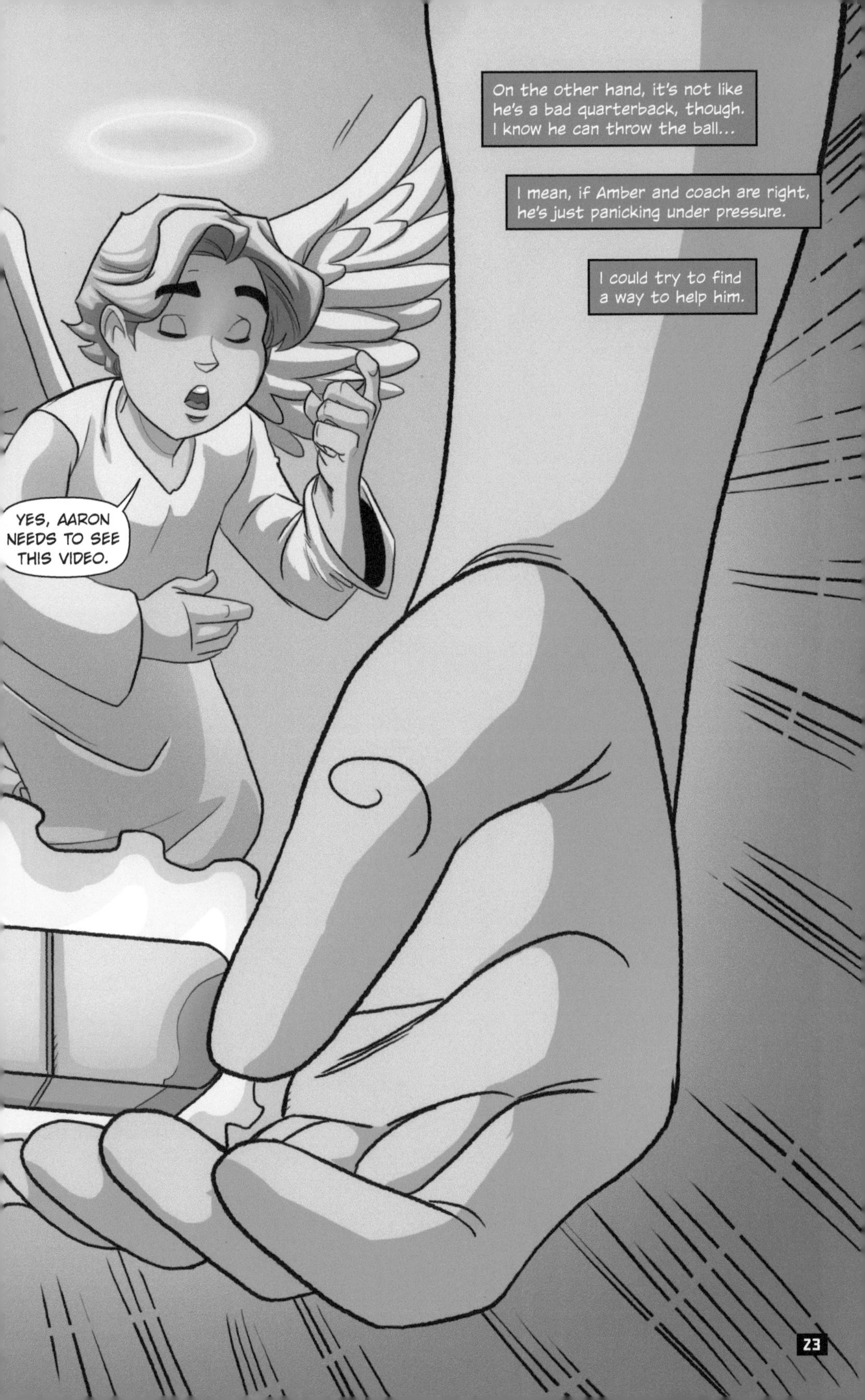
On the other hand, it's not like he's a bad quarterback, though. I know he can throw the ball...
I mean, if Amber and coach are right, he's just panicking under pressure.
I could try to find a way to help him.
YES, AARON NEEDS TO SEE THIS VIDEO.

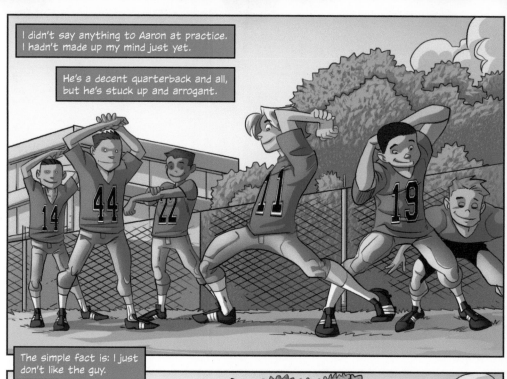

I didn't say anything to Aaron at practice. I hadn't made up my mind just yet.

He's a decent quarterback and all, but he's stuck up and arrogant.

The simple fact is: I just don't like the guy.

DUM~

Besides, what makes it my responsibility to help him?

AHEM! FOR THE GOOD OF THE TEAM!!

I mean, *besides that!*

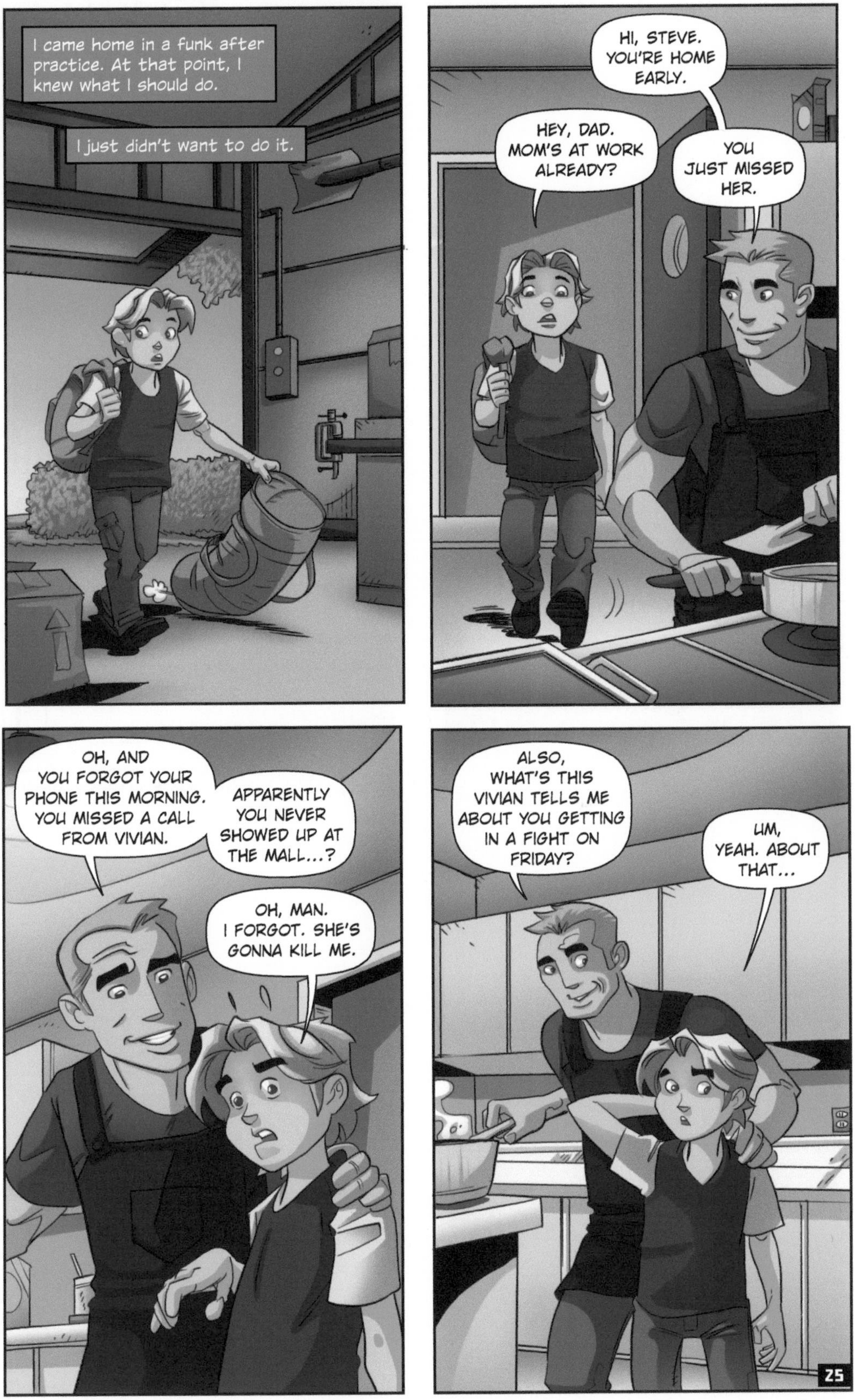

I came home in a funk after practice. At that point, I knew what I should do.
I just didn't want to do it.
HI, STEVE. YOU'RE HOME EARLY.
HEY, DAD. MOM'S AT WORK ALREADY?
YOU JUST MISSED HER.
OH, AND YOU FORGOT YOUR PHONE THIS MORNING. YOU MISSED A CALL FROM VIVIAN.
APPARENTLY YOU NEVER SHOWED UP AT THE MALL...?
OH, MAN. I FORGOT. SHE'S GONNA KILL ME.
ALSO, WHAT'S THIS VIVIAN TELLS ME ABOUT YOU GETTING IN A FIGHT ON FRIDAY?
UM, YEAH. ABOUT THAT...

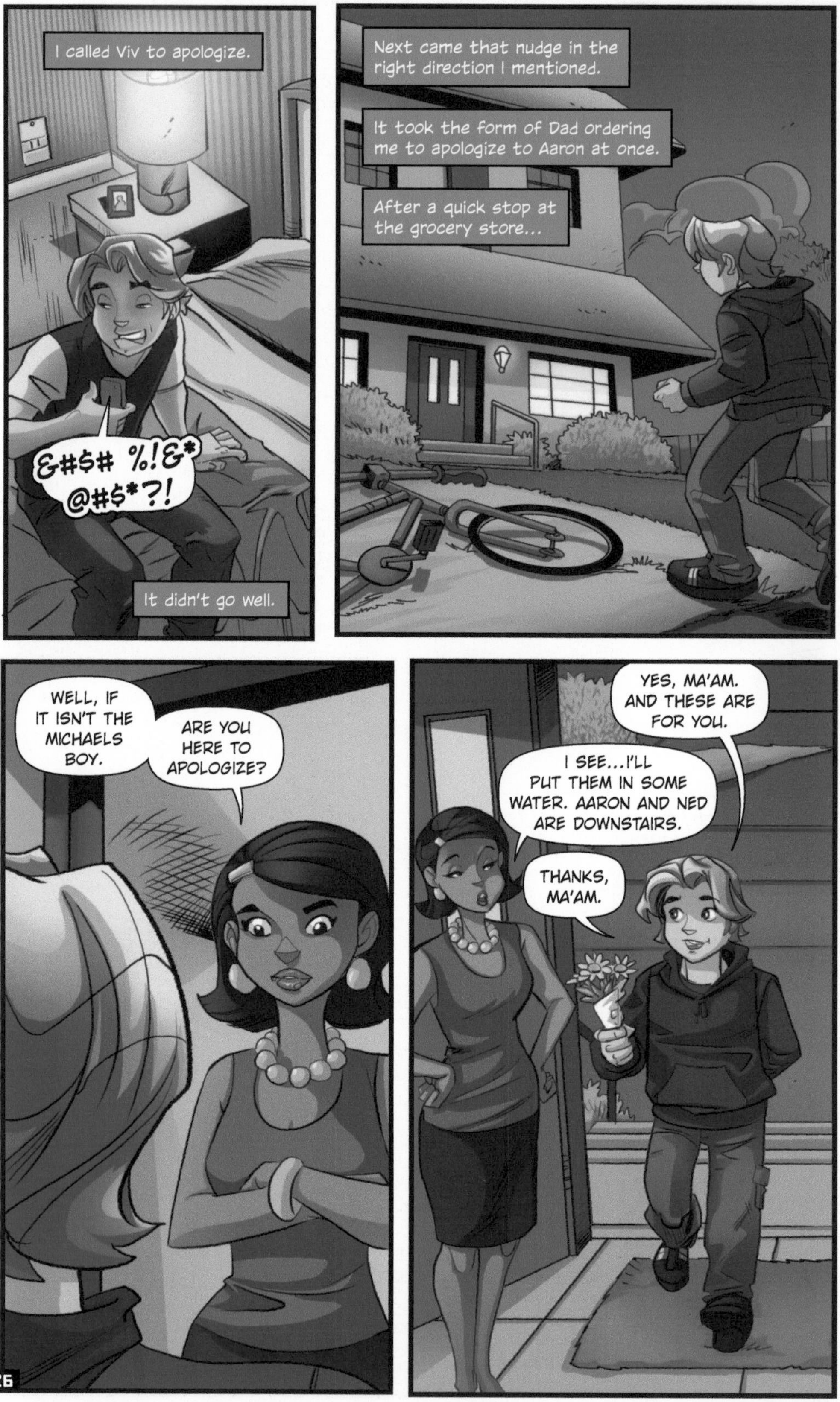
I called Viv to apologize.
&#$# %!&* @#$*?!
It didn't go well.
Next came that nudge in the right direction I mentioned.
It took the form of Dad ordering me to apologize to Aaron at once.
After a quick stop at the grocery store...
WELL, IF IT ISN'T THE MICHAELS BOY.
ARE YOU HERE TO APOLOGIZE?
YES, MA'AM. AND THESE ARE FOR YOU.
I SEE...I'LL PUT THEM IN SOME WATER. AARON AND NED ARE DOWNSTAIRS.
THANKS, MA'AM.

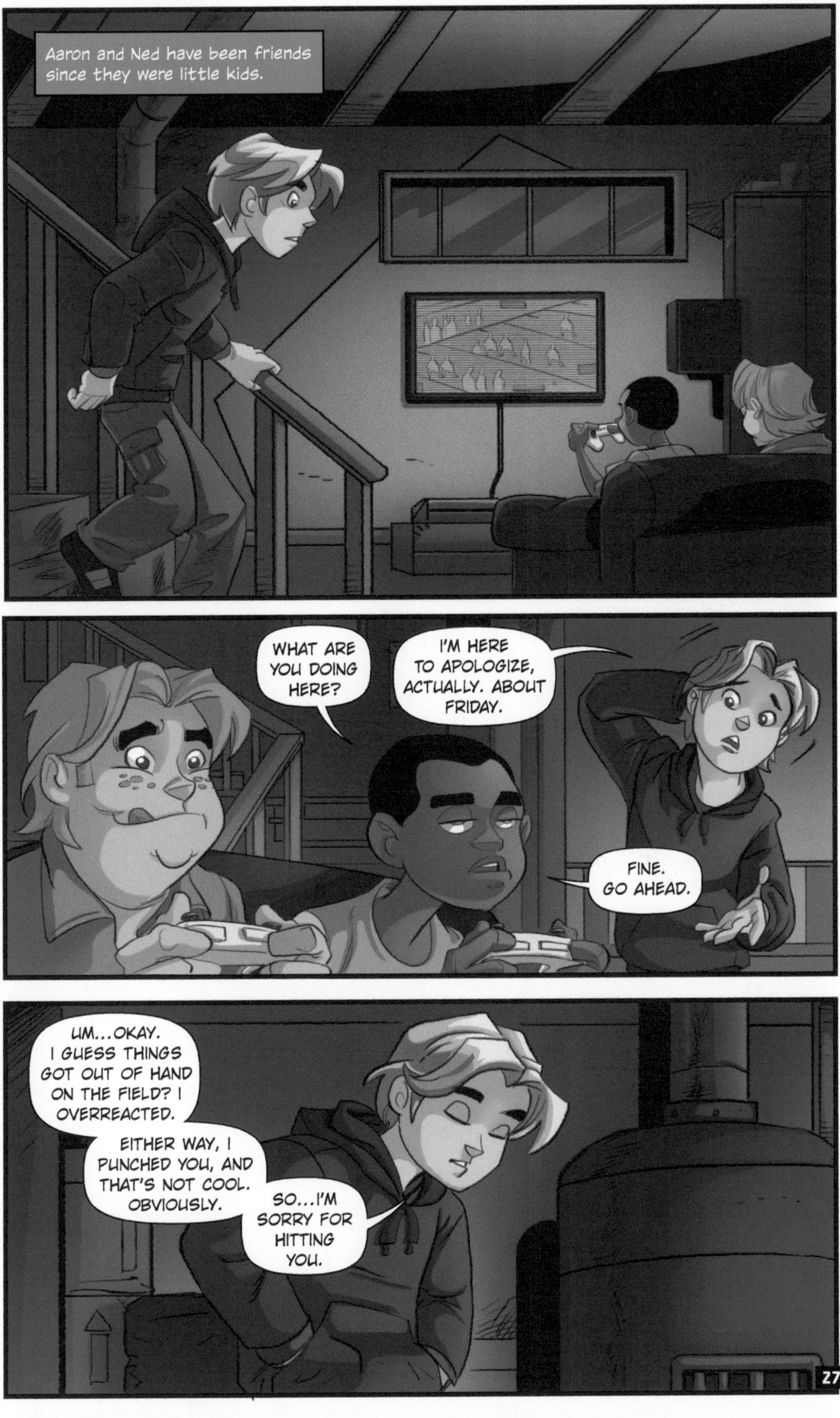
Aaron and Ned have been friends since they were little kids.
WHAT ARE YOU DOING HERE?
I'M HERE TO APOLOGIZE, ACTUALLY. ABOUT FRIDAY.
FINE. GO AHEAD.
UM...OKAY. I GUESS THINGS GOT OUT OF HAND ON THE FIELD? I OVERREACTED.
EITHER WAY, I PUNCHED YOU, AND THAT'S NOT COOL. OBVIOUSLY.
SO...I'M SORRY FOR HITTING YOU.

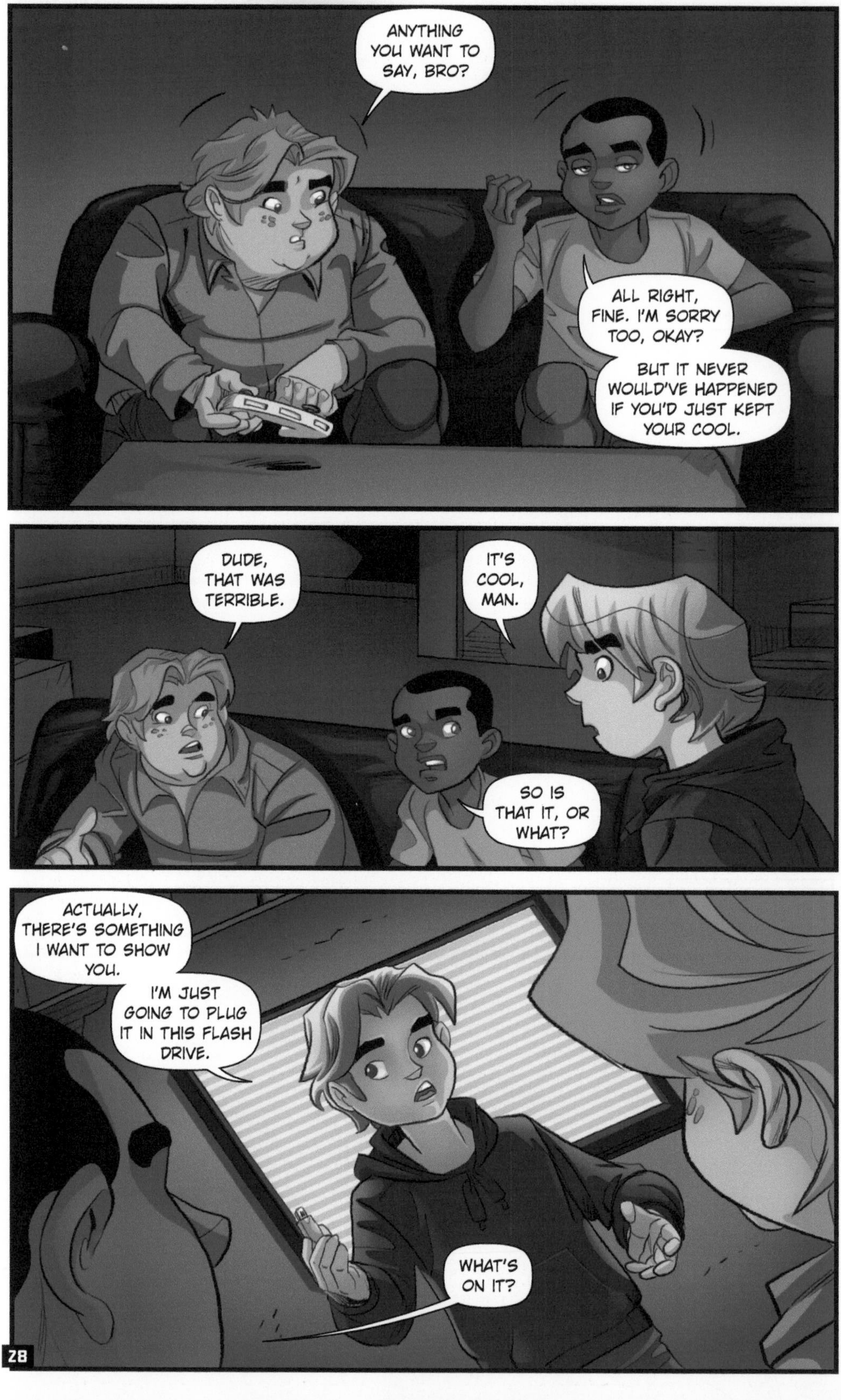
ANYTHING YOU WANT TO SAY, BRO?
ALL RIGHT, FINE. I'M SORRY TOO, OKAY?
BUT IT NEVER WOULD'VE HAPPENED IF YOU'D JUST KEPT YOUR COOL.
DUDE, THAT WAS TERRIBLE.
IT'S COOL, MAN.
SO IS THAT IT, OR WHAT?
ACTUALLY, THERE'S SOMETHING I WANT TO SHOW YOU.
I'M JUST GOING TO PLUG IT IN THIS FLASH DRIVE.
WHAT'S ON IT?

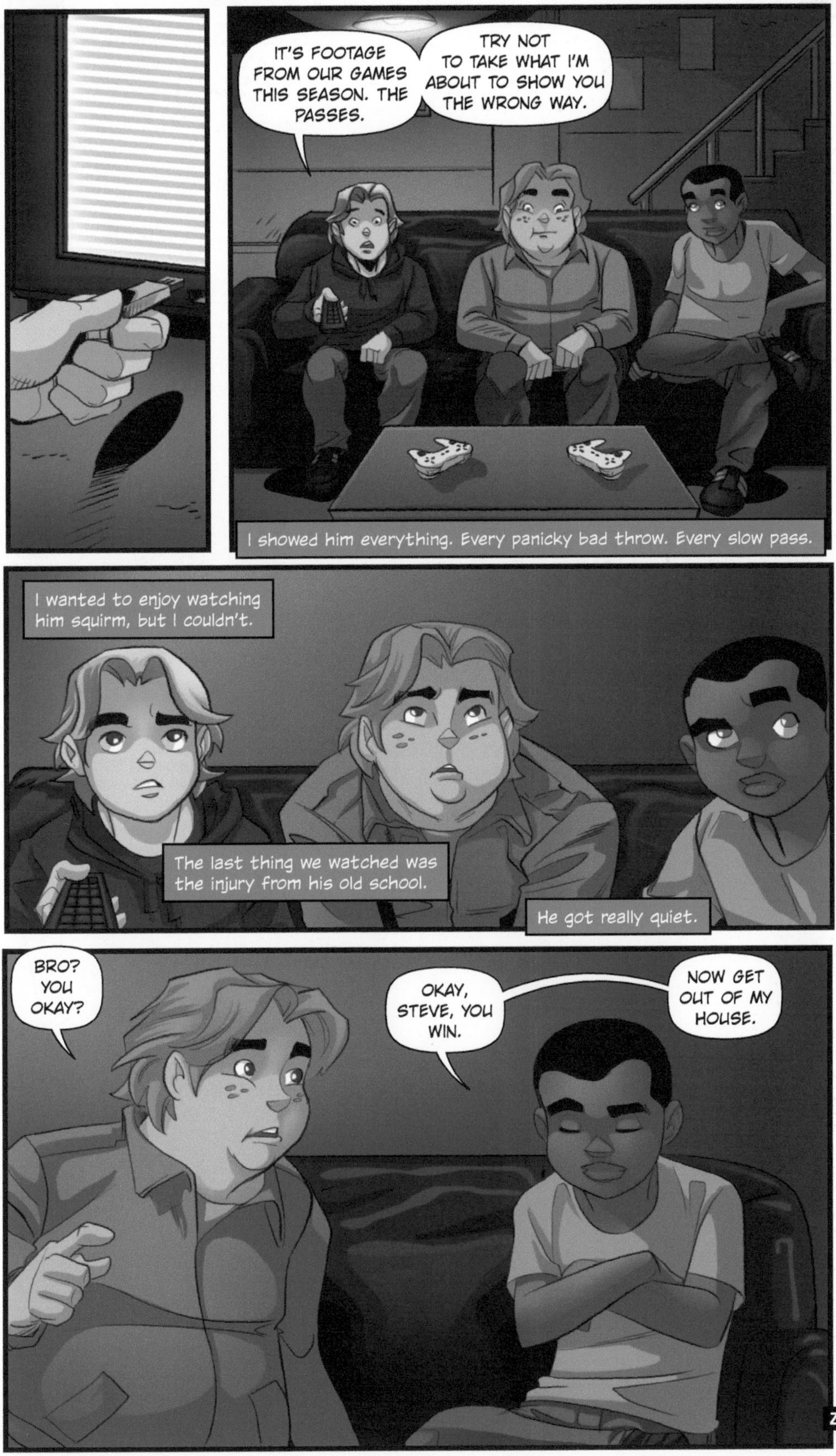
IT'S FOOTAGE FROM OUR GAMES THIS SEASON. THE PASSES.
TRY NOT TO TAKE WHAT I'M ABOUT TO SHOW YOU THE WRONG WAY.
I showed him everything. Every panicky bad throw. Every slow pass.
I wanted to enjoy watching him squirm, but I couldn't.
The last thing we watched was the injury from his old school.
He got really quiet.
BRO? YOU OKAY?
OKAY, STEVE, YOU WIN.
NOW GET OUT OF MY HOUSE.

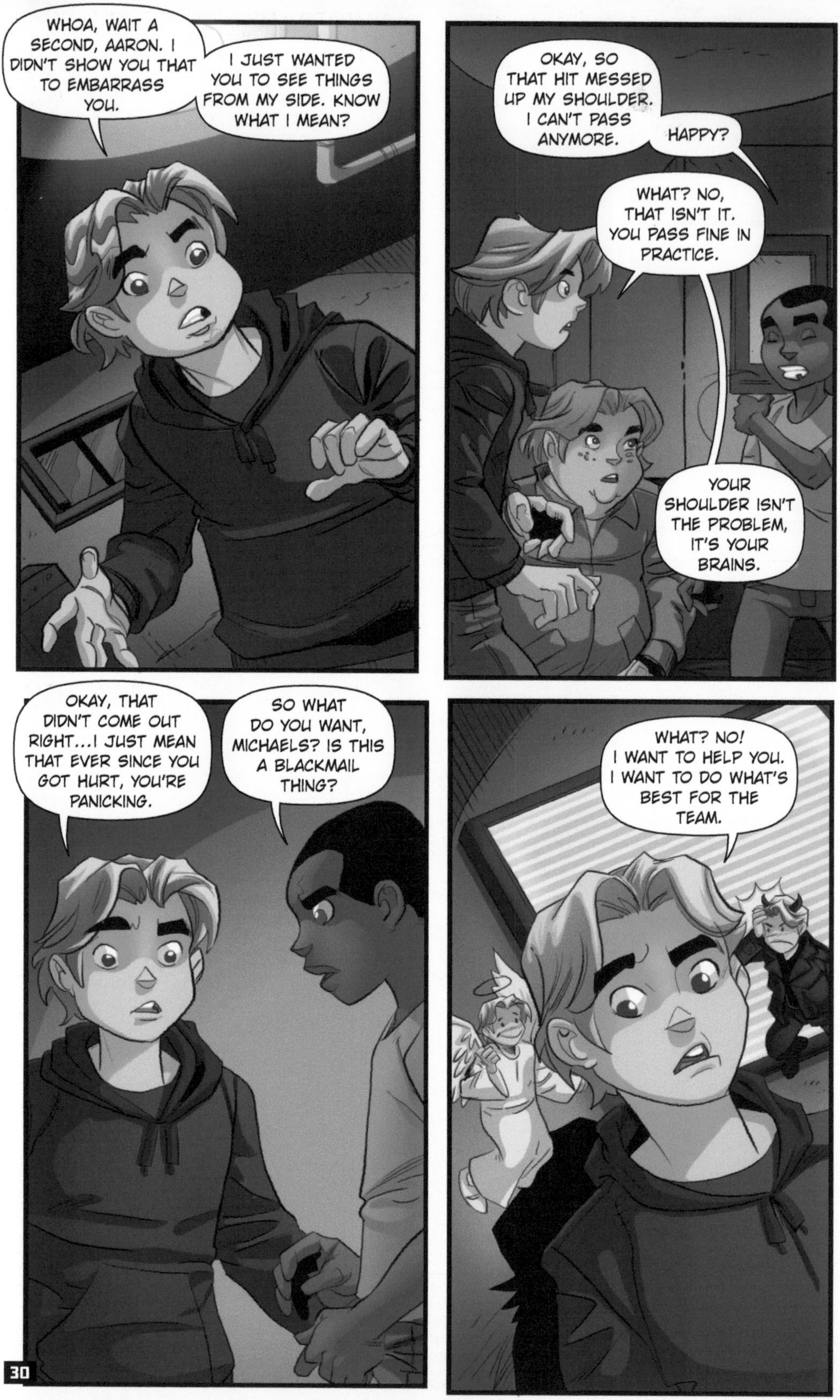
WHOA, WAIT A SECOND, AARON. I DIDN'T SHOW YOU THAT TO EMBARRASS YOU.
I JUST WANTED YOU TO SEE THINGS FROM MY SIDE. KNOW WHAT I MEAN?
OKAY, SO THAT HIT MESSED UP MY SHOULDER. I CAN'T PASS ANYMORE.
HAPPY?
WHAT? NO, THAT ISN'T IT. YOU PASS FINE IN PRACTICE.
YOUR SHOULDER ISN'T THE PROBLEM, IT'S YOUR BRAINS.
OKAY, THAT DIDN'T COME OUT RIGHT...I JUST MEAN THAT EVER SINCE YOU GOT HURT, YOU'RE PANICKING.
SO WHAT DO YOU WANT, MICHAELS? IS THIS A BLACKMAIL THING?
WHAT? NO! I WANT TO HELP YOU. I WANT TO DO WHAT'S BEST FOR THE TEAM.

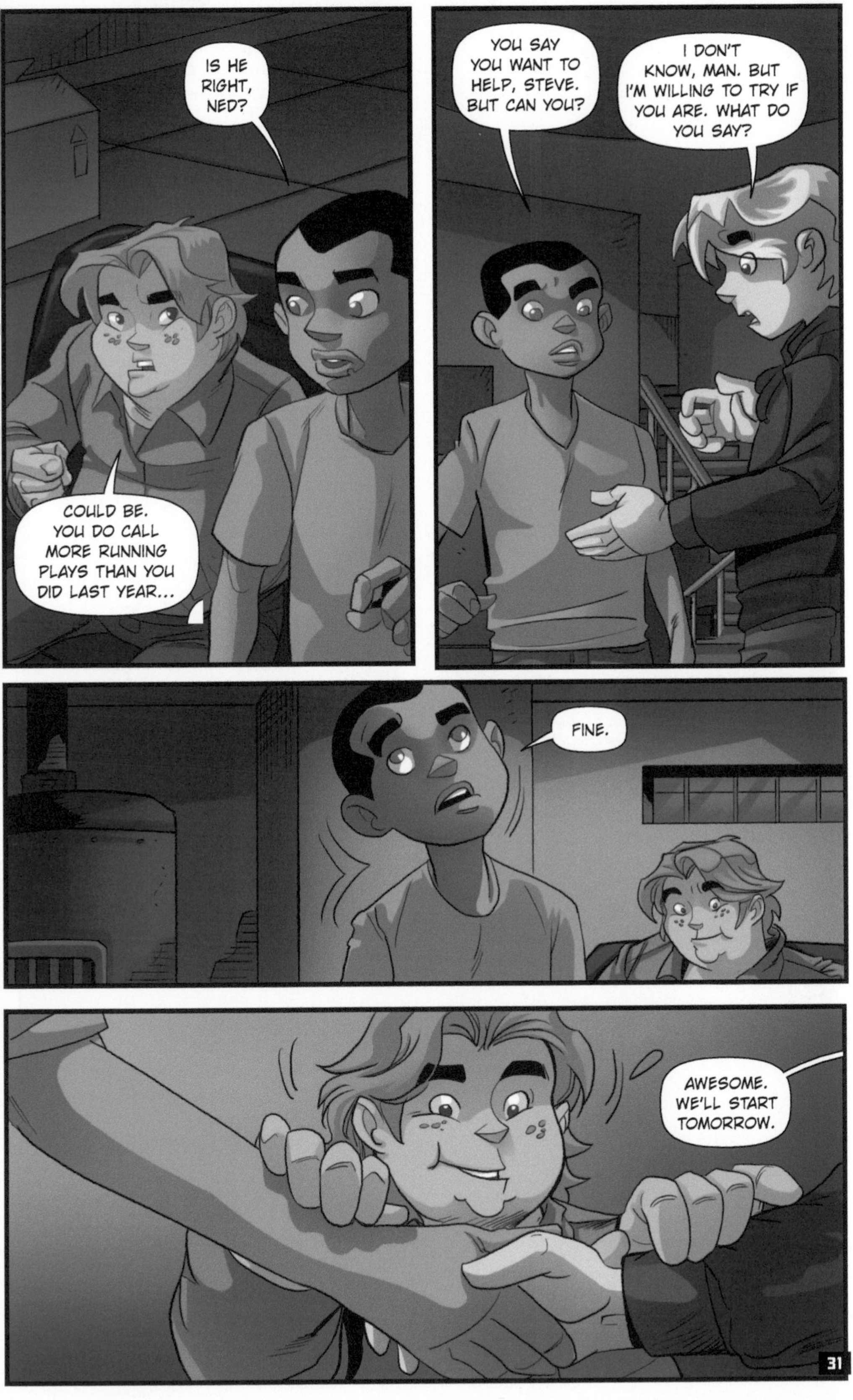
IS HE RIGHT, NED?
COULD BE. YOU DO CALL MORE RUNNING PLAYS THAN YOU DID LAST YEAR...
YOU SAY YOU WANT TO HELP, STEVE. BUT CAN YOU?
I DON'T KNOW, MAN. BUT I'M WILLING TO TRY IF YOU ARE. WHAT DO YOU SAY?
FINE.
AWESOME. WE'LL START TOMORROW.

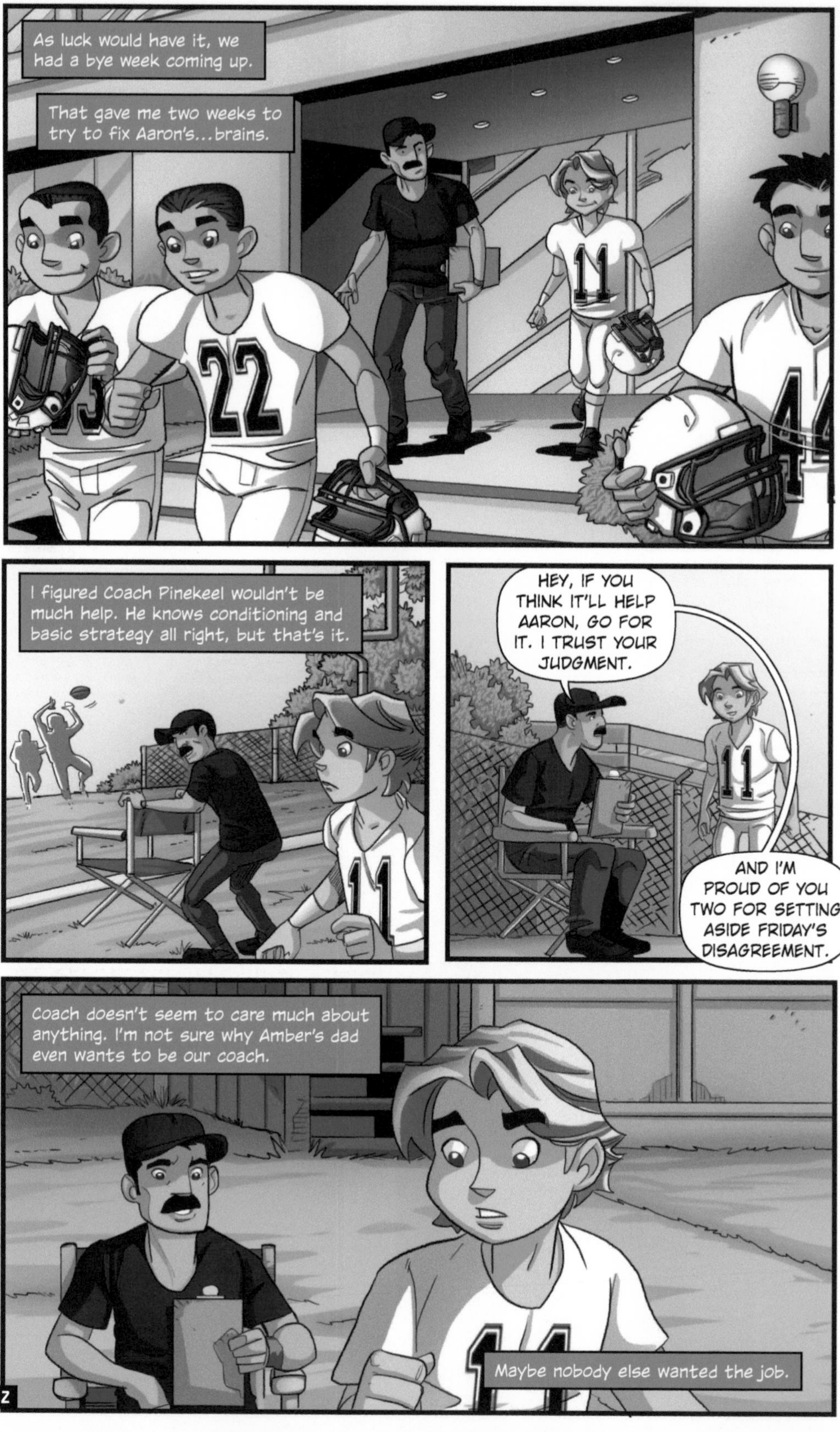
As luck would have it, we had a bye week coming up.
That gave me two weeks to try to fix Aaron's...brains.
I figured Coach Pinekeel wouldn't be much help. He knows conditioning and basic strategy all right, but that's it.
HEY, IF YOU THINK IT'LL HELP AARON, GO FOR IT. I TRUST YOUR JUDGMENT.
AND I'M PROUD OF YOU TWO FOR SETTING ASIDE FRIDAY'S DISAGREEMENT.
Coach doesn't seem to care much about anything. I'm not sure why Amber's dad even wants to be our coach.
Maybe nobody else wanted the job.

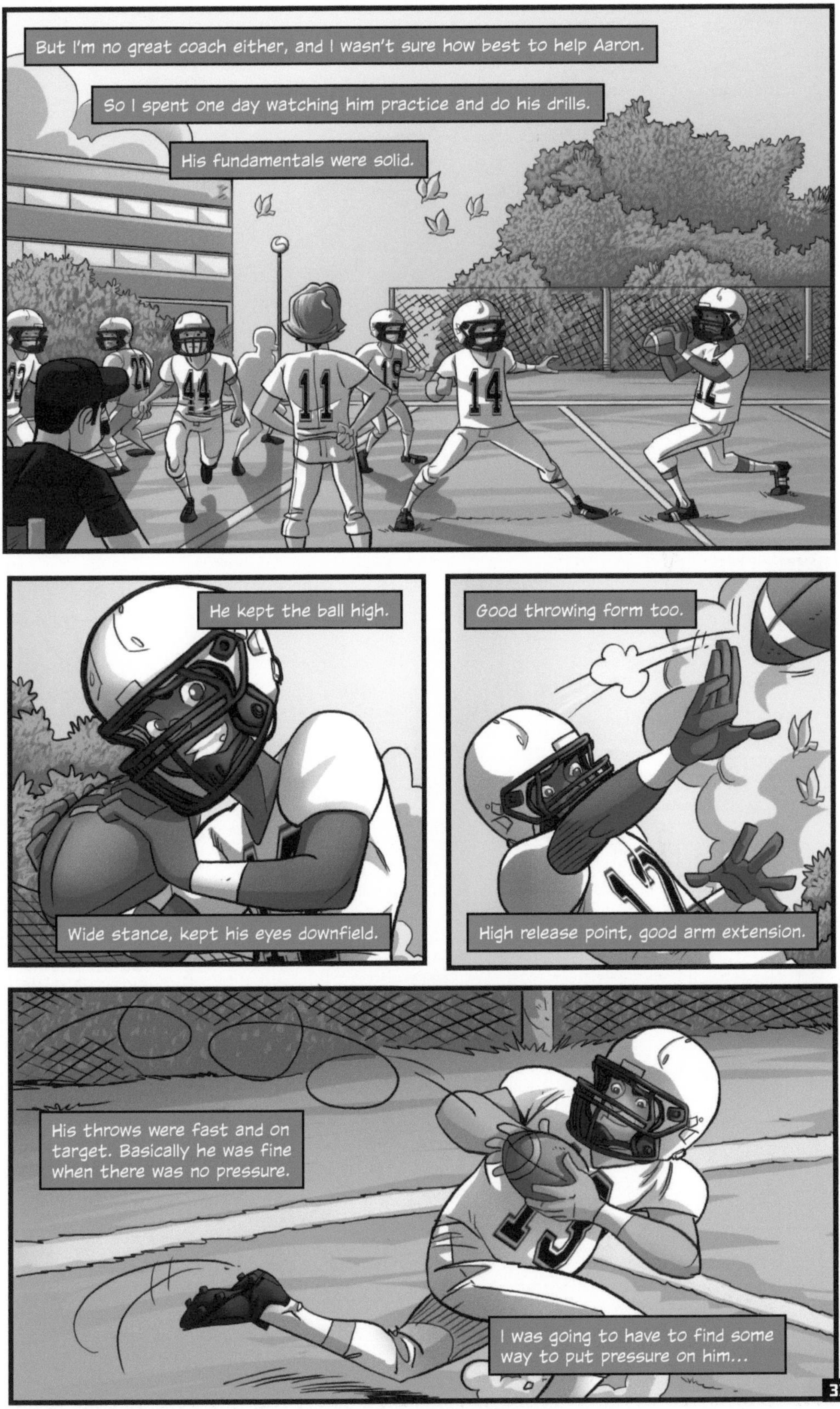
But I'm no great coach either, and I wasn't sure how best to help Aaron.
So I spent one day watching him practice and do his drills.
His fundamentals were solid.
He kept the ball high.
Wide stance, kept his eyes downfield.
Good throwing form too.
High release point, good arm extension.
His throws were fast and on target. Basically he was fine when there was no pressure.
I was going to have to find some way to put pressure on him...

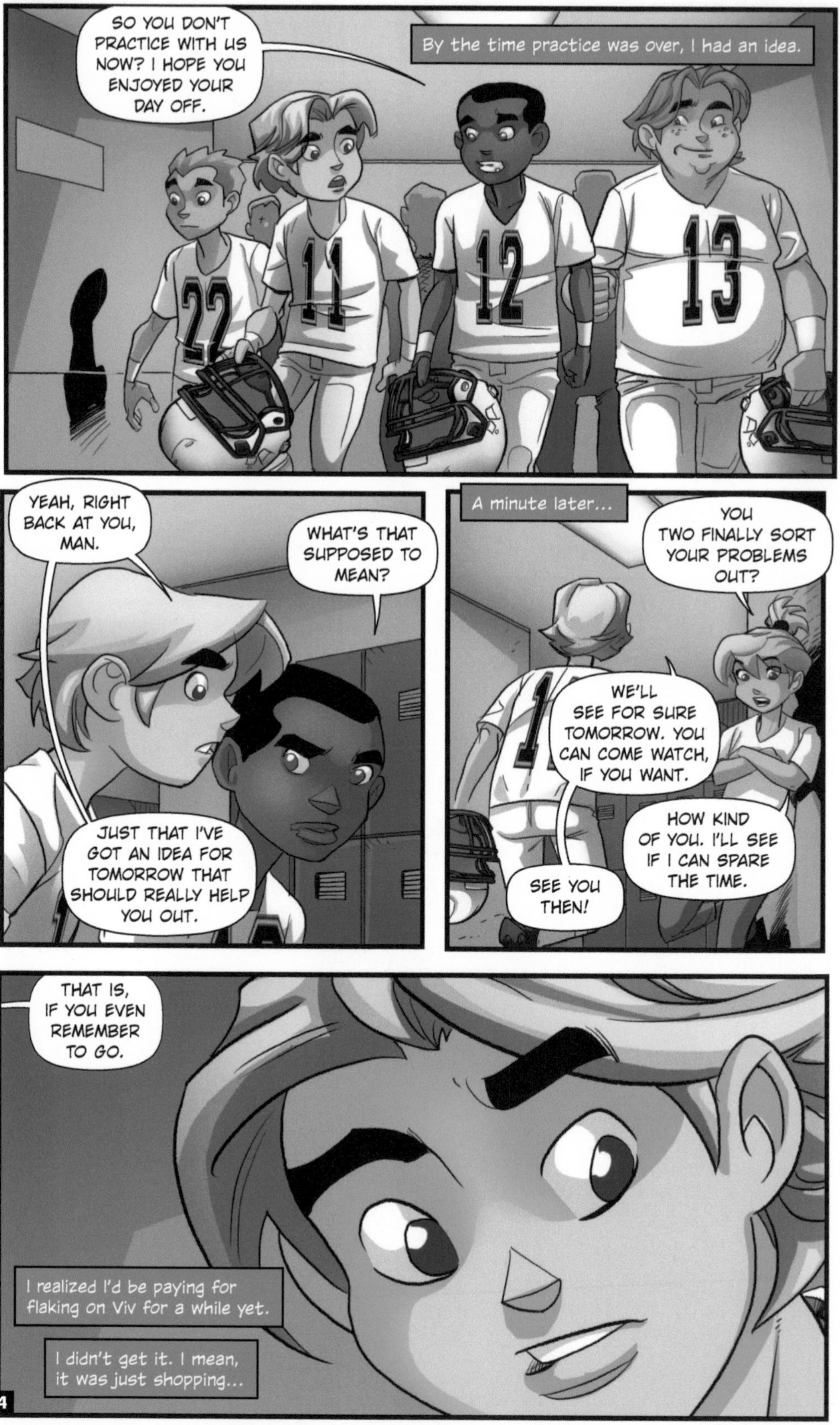

By the time practice was over, I had an idea.
SO YOU DON'T PRACTICE WITH US NOW? I HOPE YOU ENJOYED YOUR DAY OFF.
YEAH, RIGHT BACK AT YOU, MAN.
WHAT'S THAT SUPPOSED TO MEAN?
JUST THAT I'VE GOT AN IDEA FOR TOMORROW THAT SHOULD REALLY HELP YOU OUT.
A minute later...
YOU TWO FINALLY SORT YOUR PROBLEMS OUT?
WE'LL SEE FOR SURE TOMORROW. YOU CAN COME WATCH, IF YOU WANT.
HOW KIND OF YOU. I'LL SEE IF I CAN SPARE THE TIME.
SEE YOU THEN!
THAT IS, IF YOU EVEN REMEMBER TO GO.
I realized I'd be paying for flaking on Viv for a while yet.
I didn't get it. I mean, it was just shopping...

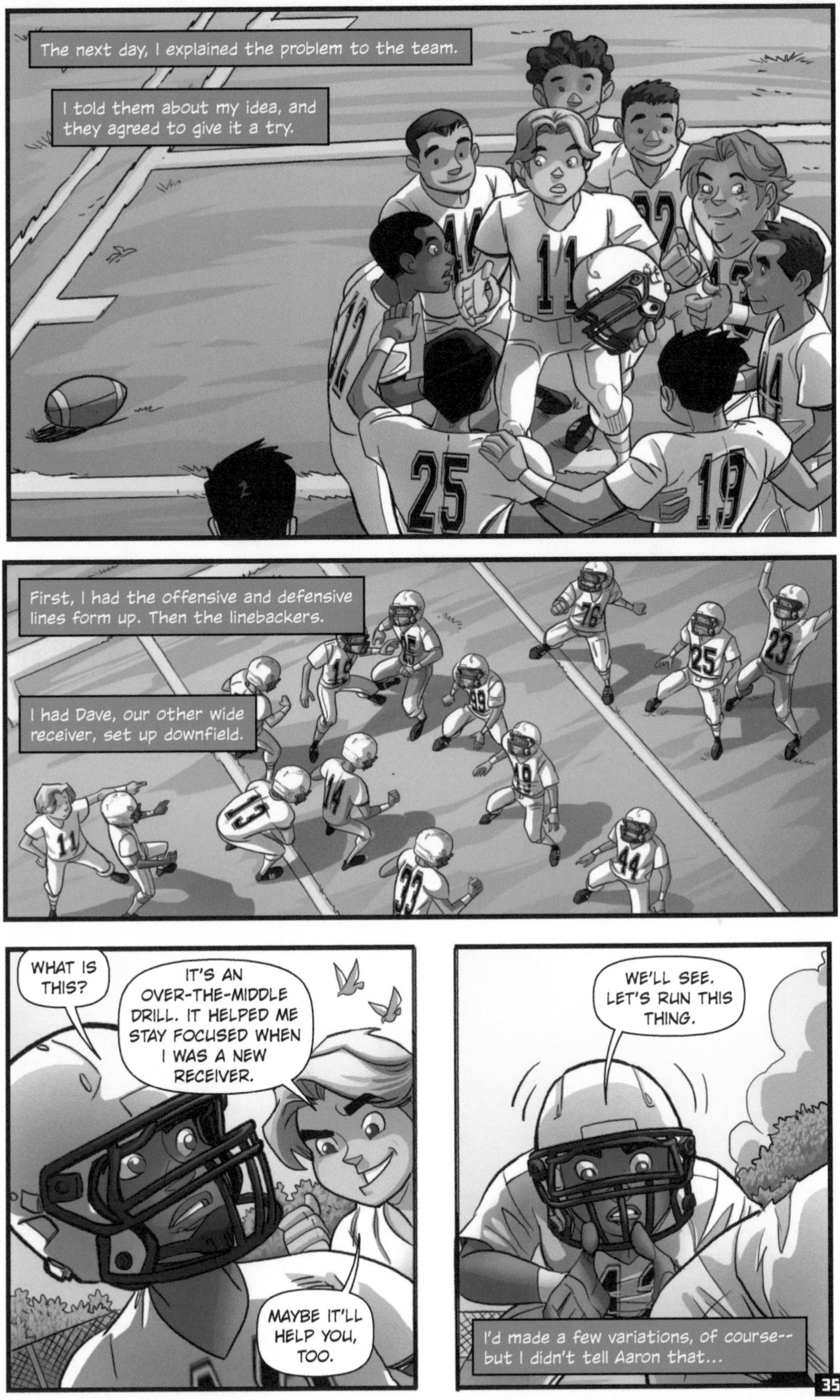
The next day, I explained the problem to the team.
I told them about my idea, and they agreed to give it a try.
First, I had the offensive and defensive lines form up. Then the linebackers.
I had Dave, our other wide receiver, set up downfield.
WHAT IS THIS?
IT'S AN OVER-THE-MIDDLE DRILL. IT HELPED ME STAY FOCUSED WHEN I WAS A NEW RECEIVER.
MAYBE IT'LL HELP YOU, TOO.
WE'LL SEE. LET'S RUN THIS THING.
I'd made a few variations, of course--but I didn't tell Aaron that...

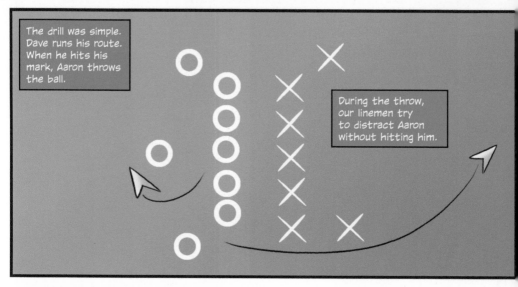

The drill was simple. Dave runs his route. When he hits his mark, Aaron throws the ball.

During the throw, our linemen try to distract Aaron without hitting him.

The idea is to train the quarterback to keep his cool despite distractions.

HIKE!

After I'm done with him, Aaron should be able to ignore just about anything.

NICE TOSS, AARON!

I let him get off the first pass without pressure...

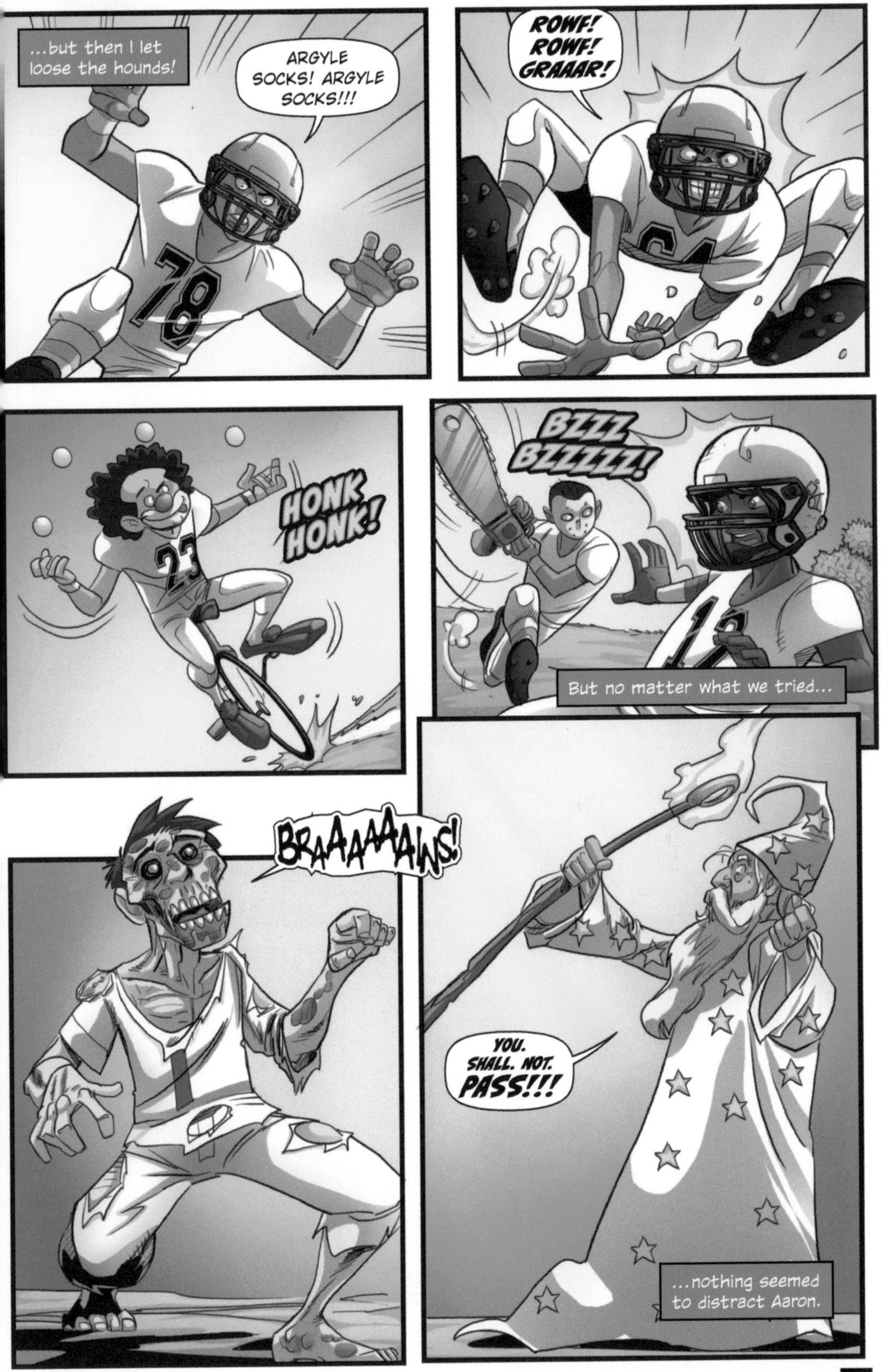
...but then I let loose the hounds!
ARGYLE SOCKS! ARGYLE SOCKS!!!
ROWF! ROWF! GRAAAR!
HONK HONK!
BZZZ BZZZZZ!
But no matter what we tried...
BRAAAAAAINS!
YOU. SHALL. NOT. PASS!!!
...nothing seemed to distract Aaron.

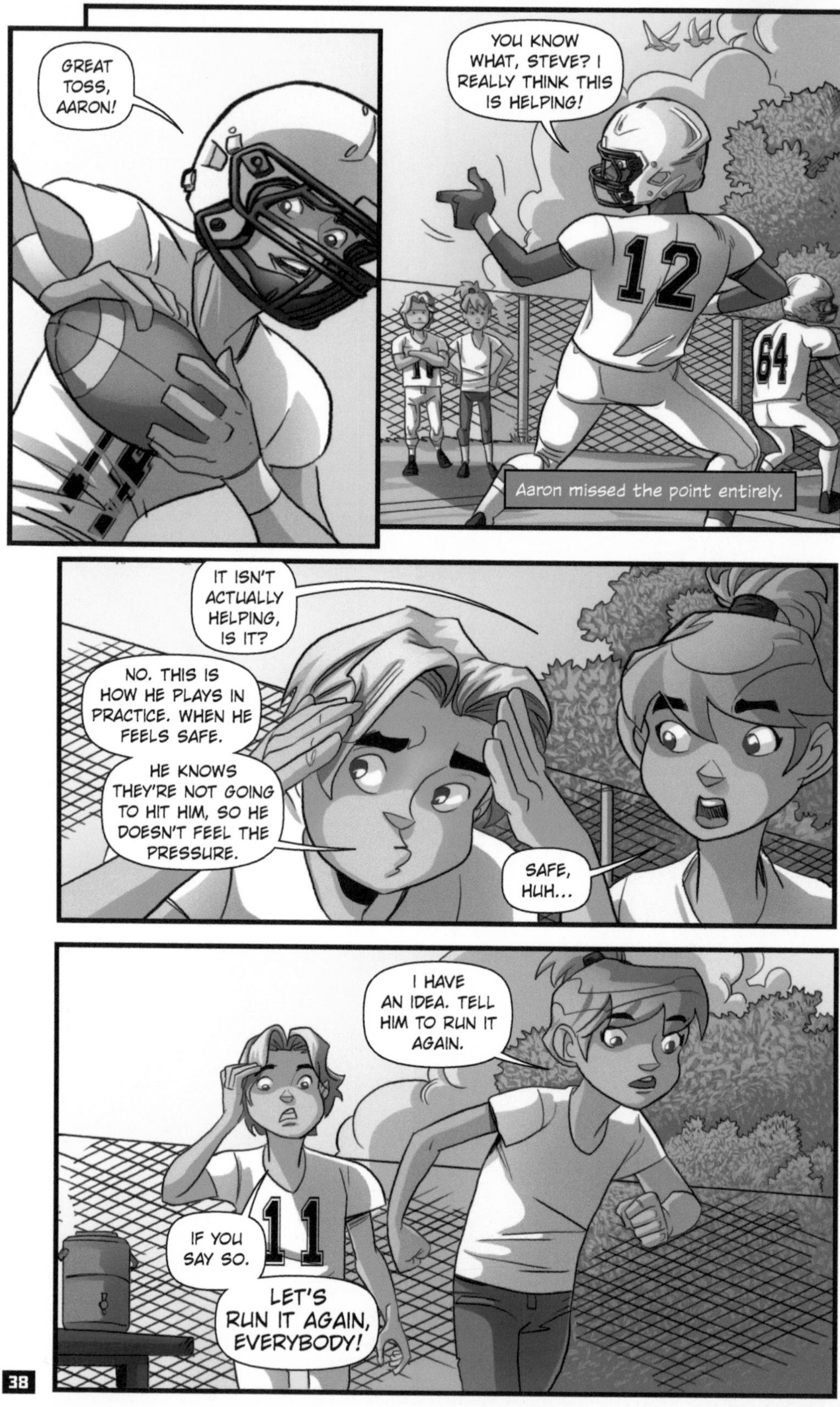
GREAT TOSS, AARON!
YOU KNOW WHAT, STEVE? I REALLY THINK THIS IS HELPING!
Aaron missed the point entirely.
IT ISN'T ACTUALLY HELPING, IS IT?
NO. THIS IS HOW HE PLAYS IN PRACTICE. WHEN HE FEELS SAFE.
HE KNOWS THEY'RE NOT GOING TO HIT HIM, SO HE DOESN'T FEEL THE PRESSURE.
SAFE, HUH...
I HAVE AN IDEA. TELL HIM TO RUN IT AGAIN.
IF YOU SAY SO.
LET'S RUN IT AGAIN, EVERYBODY!

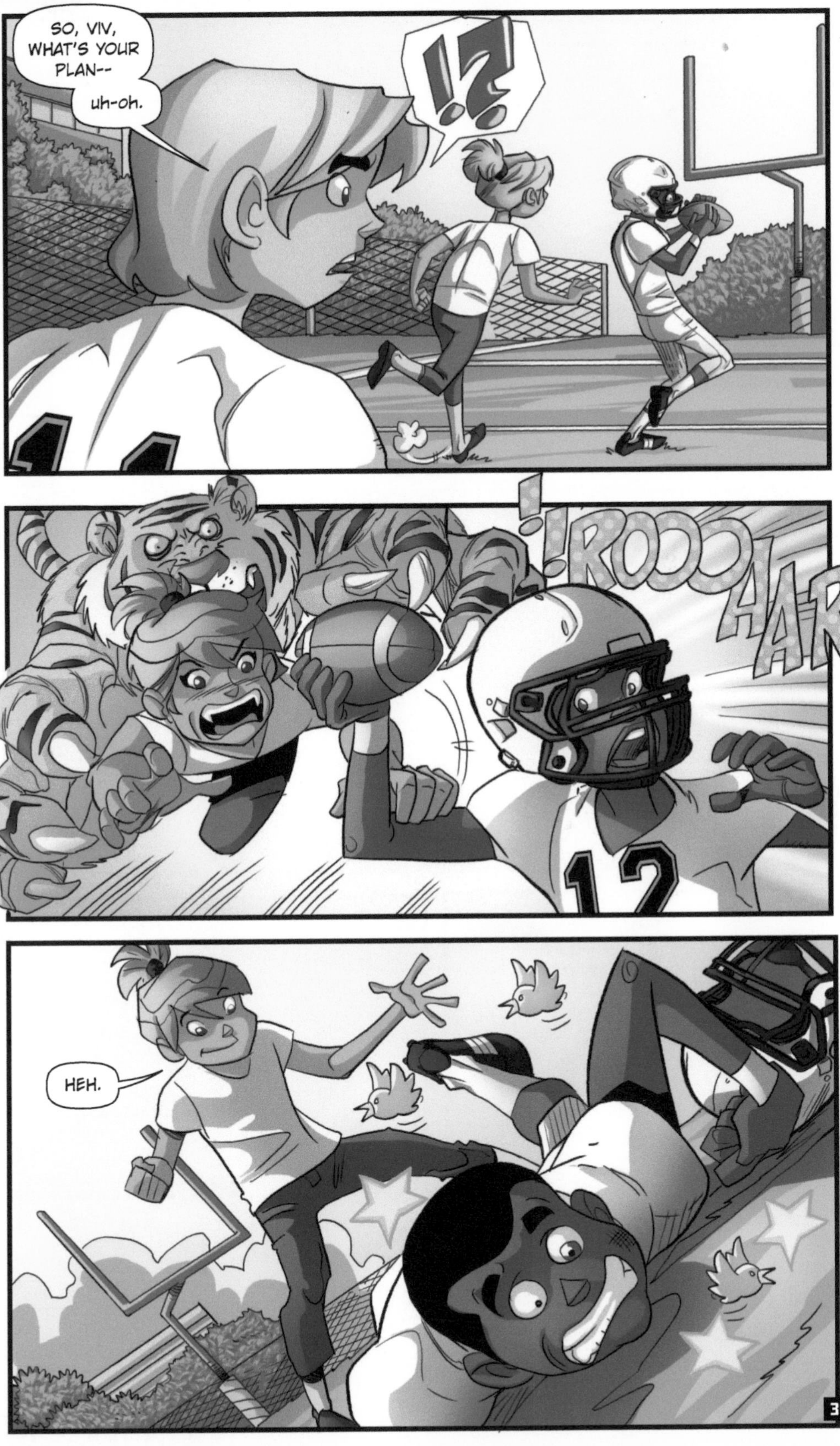

SO, VIV, WHAT'S YOUR PLAN--
uh-oh.
!?
ROOOAAR
HEH.

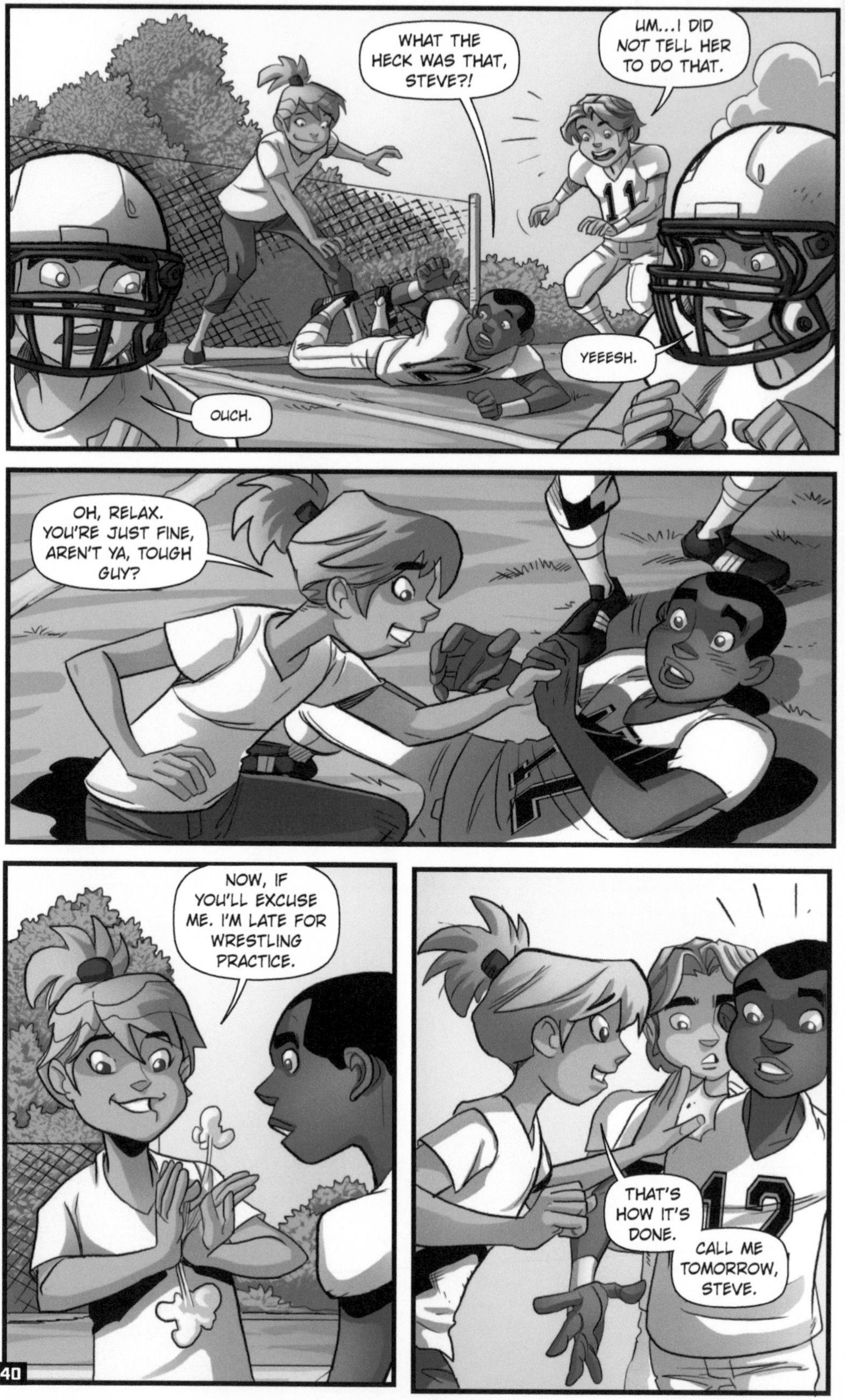
WHAT THE HECK WAS THAT, STEVE?!
UM...I DID NOT TELL HER TO DO THAT.
YEEESH.
OUCH.
OH, RELAX. YOU'RE JUST FINE, AREN'T YA, TOUGH GUY?
NOW, IF YOU'LL EXCUSE ME. I'M LATE FOR WRESTLING PRACTICE.
THAT'S HOW IT'S DONE.
CALL ME TOMORROW, STEVE.

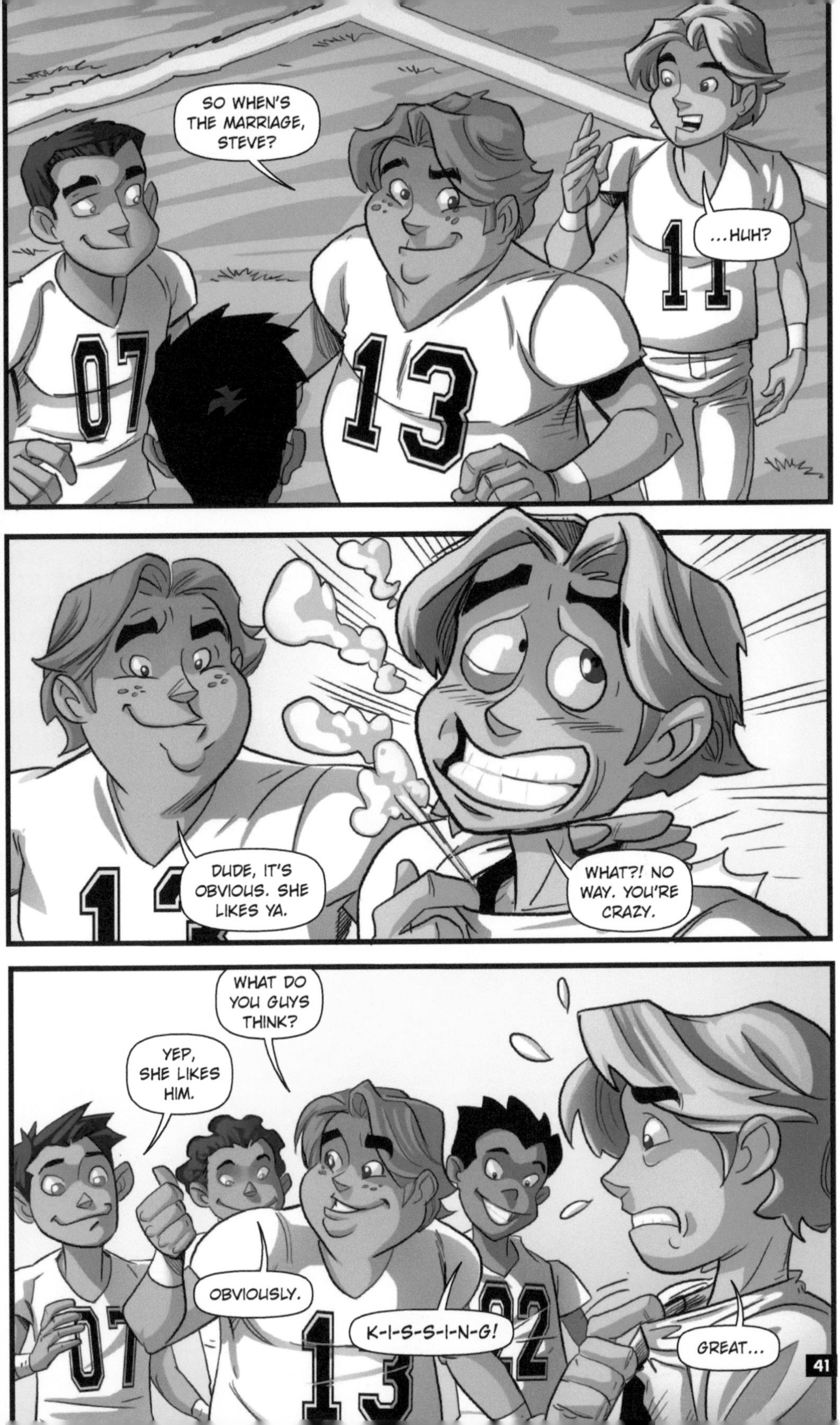
SO WHEN'S THE MARRIAGE, STEVE?
...HUH?
DUDE, IT'S OBVIOUS. SHE LIKES YA.
WHAT?! NO WAY. YOU'RE CRAZY.
WHAT DO YOU GUYS THINK?
YEP, SHE LIKES HIM.
OBVIOUSLY.
K-I-S-S-I-N-G!
GREAT...

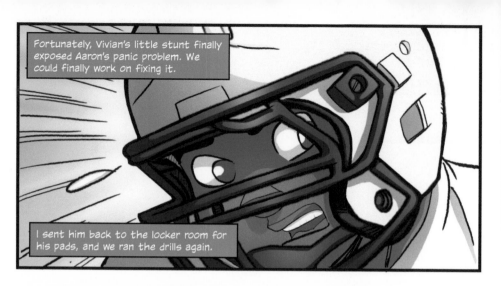

Fortunately, Vivian's little stunt finally exposed Aaron's panic problem. We could finally work on fixing it.

I sent him back to the locker room for his pads, and we ran the drills again.

Now the defensemen could hit Aaron if he still had the ball.

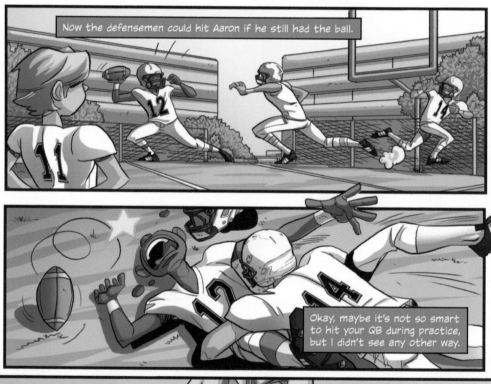

Okay, maybe it's not so smart to hit your QB during practice, but I didn't see any other way.

And I kinda enjoyed it.

Excellent...

Just a little bit.

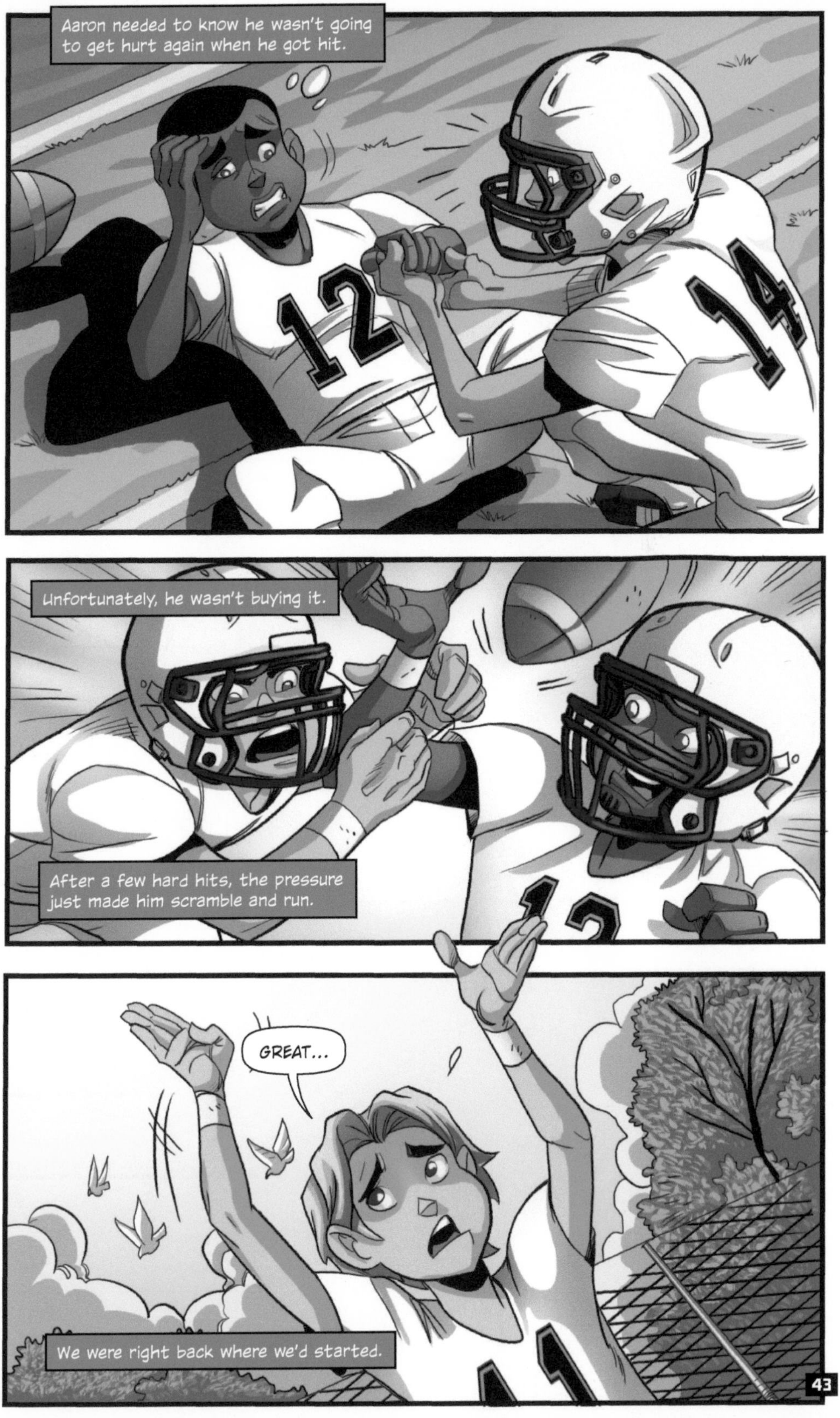
Aaron needed to know he wasn't going to get hurt again when he got hit.
Unfortunately, he wasn't buying it.
After a few hard hits, the pressure just made him scramble and run.
GREAT...
We were right back where we'd started.

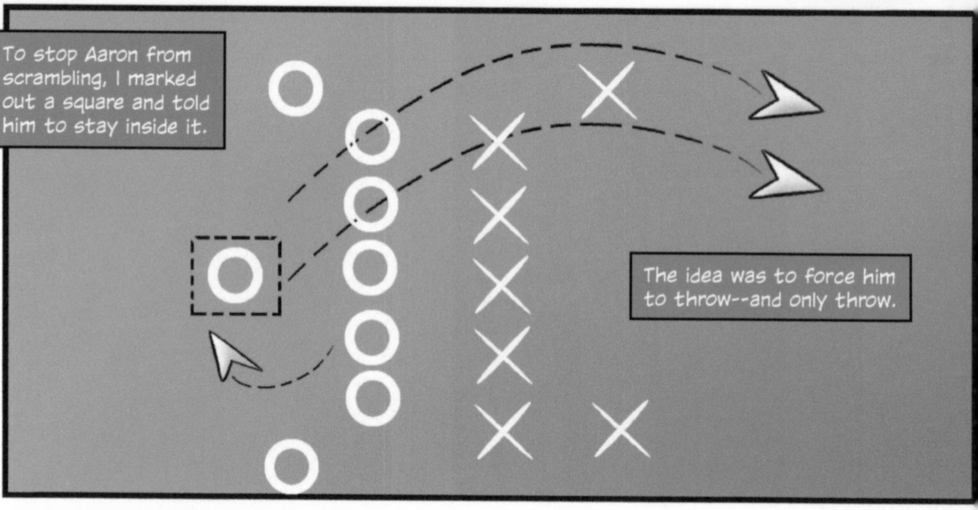
To stop Aaron from scrambling, I marked out a square and told him to stay inside it.
The idea was to force him to throw--and only throw.

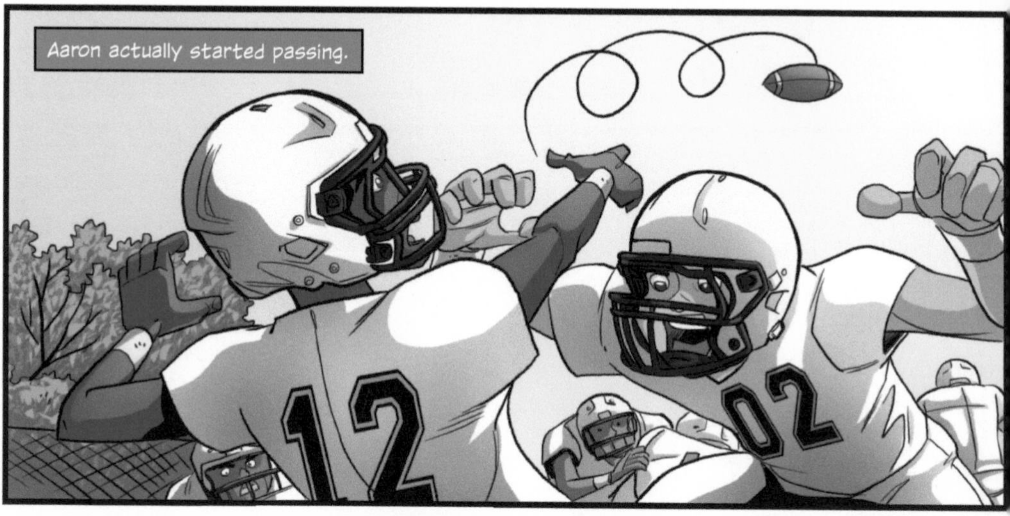
Aaron actually started passing.
12
02

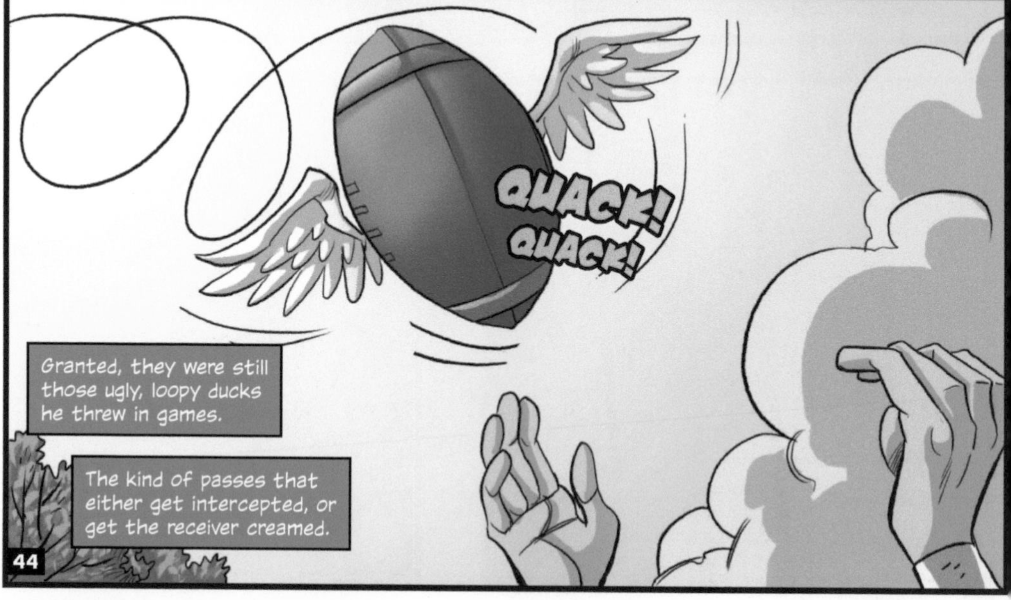
QUACK!
QUACK!
Granted, they were still those ugly, loopy ducks he threw in games.
The kind of passes that either get intercepted, or get the receiver creamed.

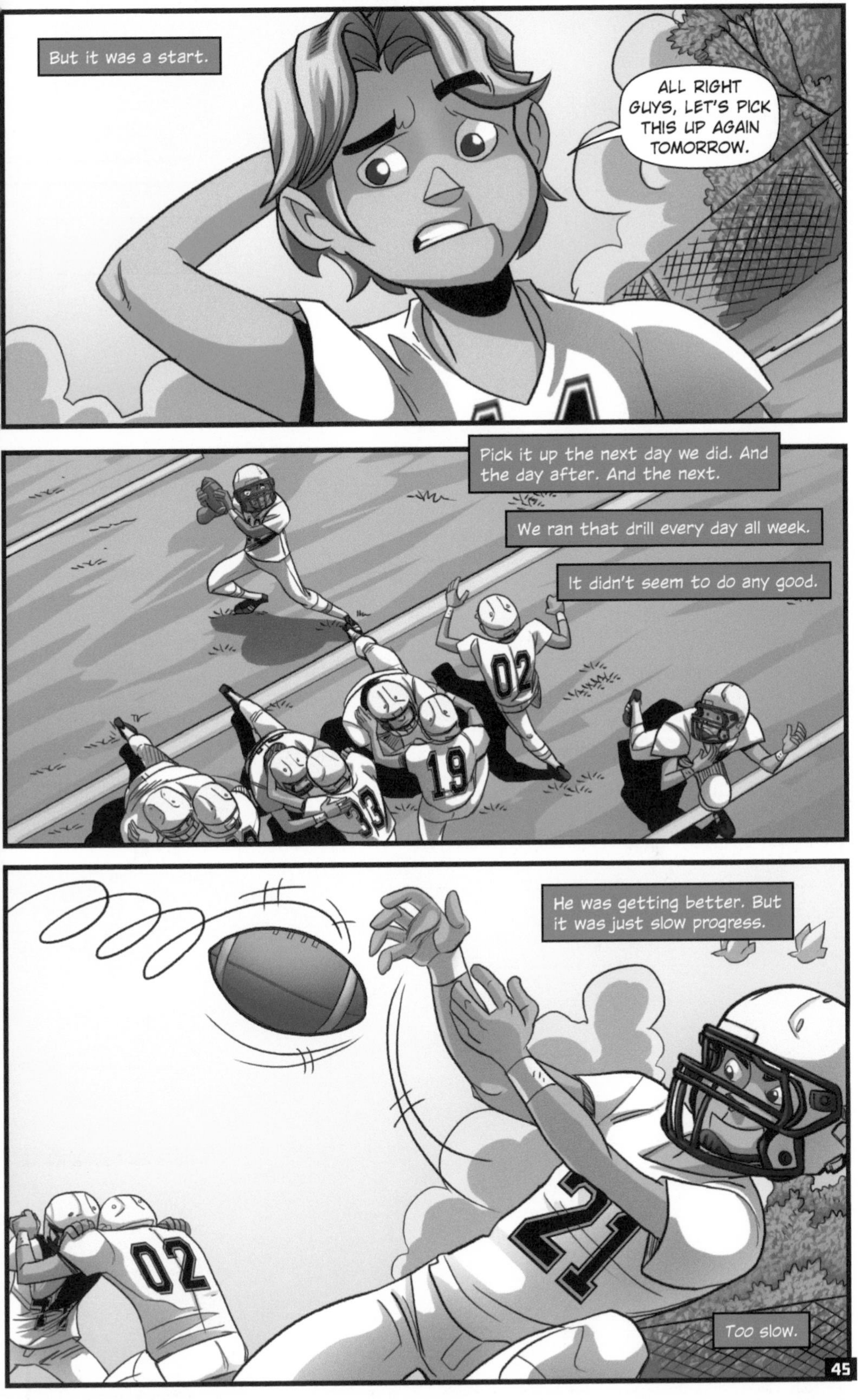
But it was a start.
ALL RIGHT GUYS, LET'S PICK THIS UP AGAIN TOMORROW.
Pick it up the next day we did. And the day after. And the next.
We ran that drill every day all week.
It didn't seem to do any good.
02
19
33
He was getting better. But it was just slow progress.
21
02
Too slow.

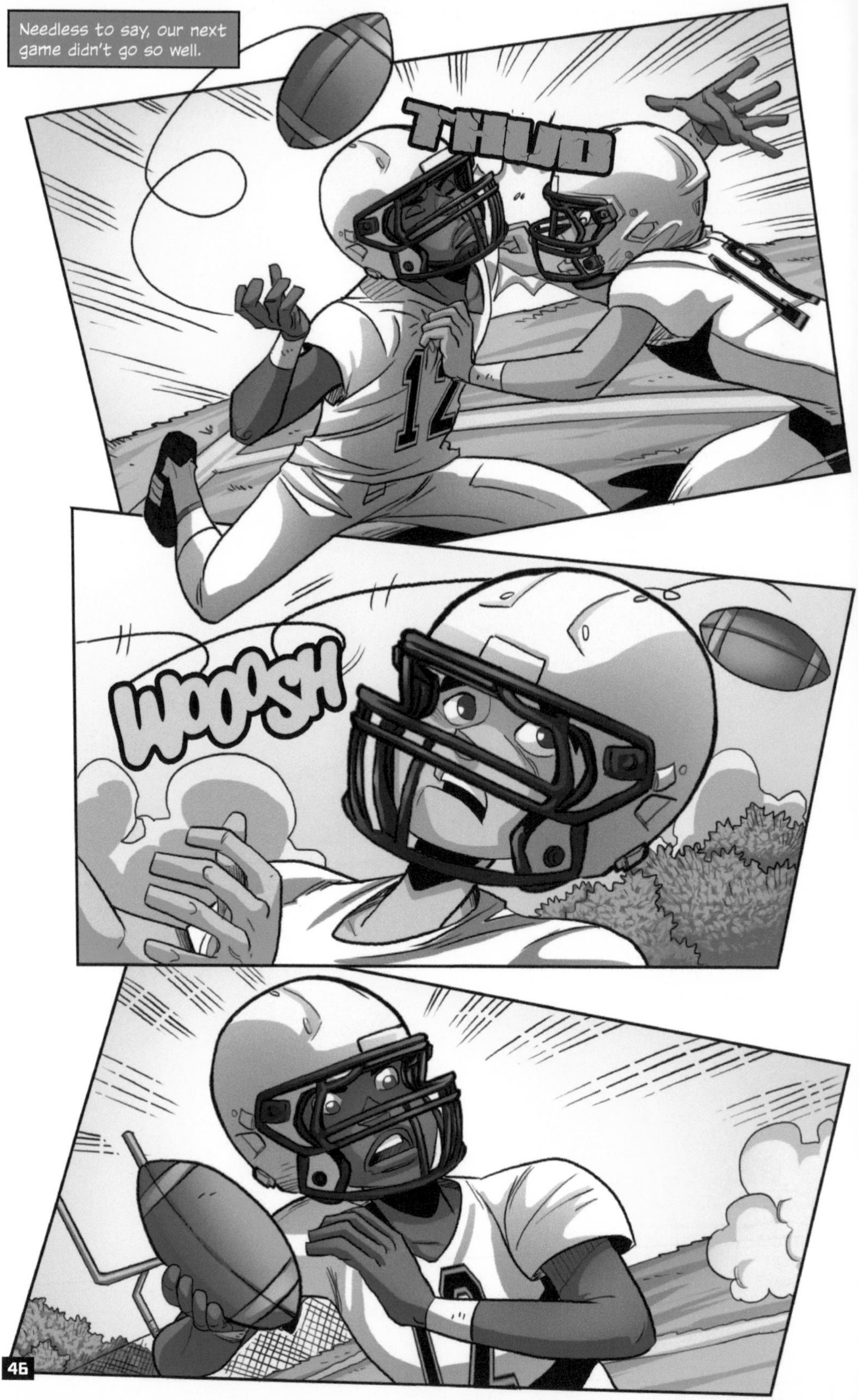
Needless to say, our next game didn't go so well.
THUD
WOOOSH

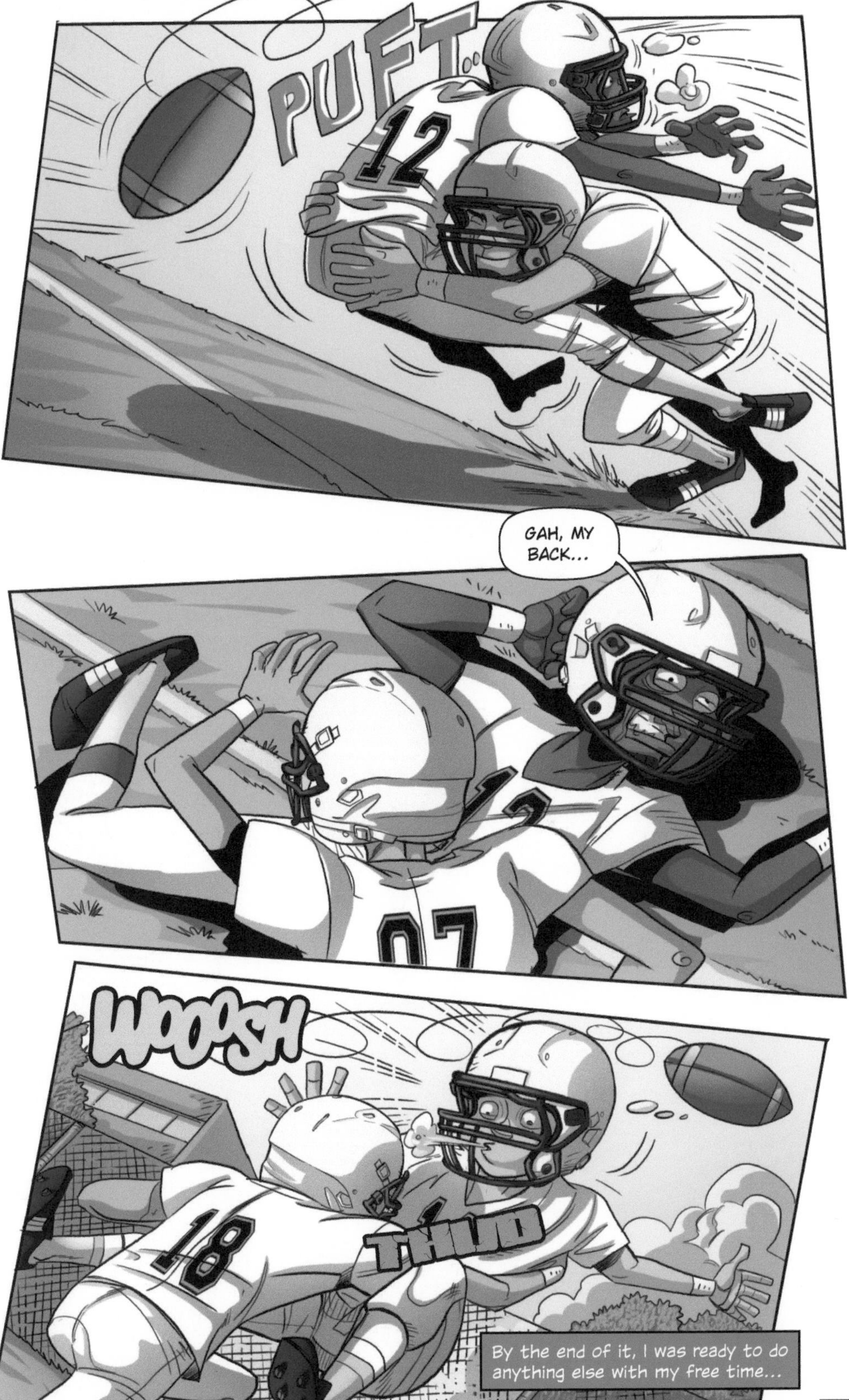
PUFT
GAH, MY BACK...
WOOOSH
THUD
By the end of it, I was ready to do anything else with my free time...

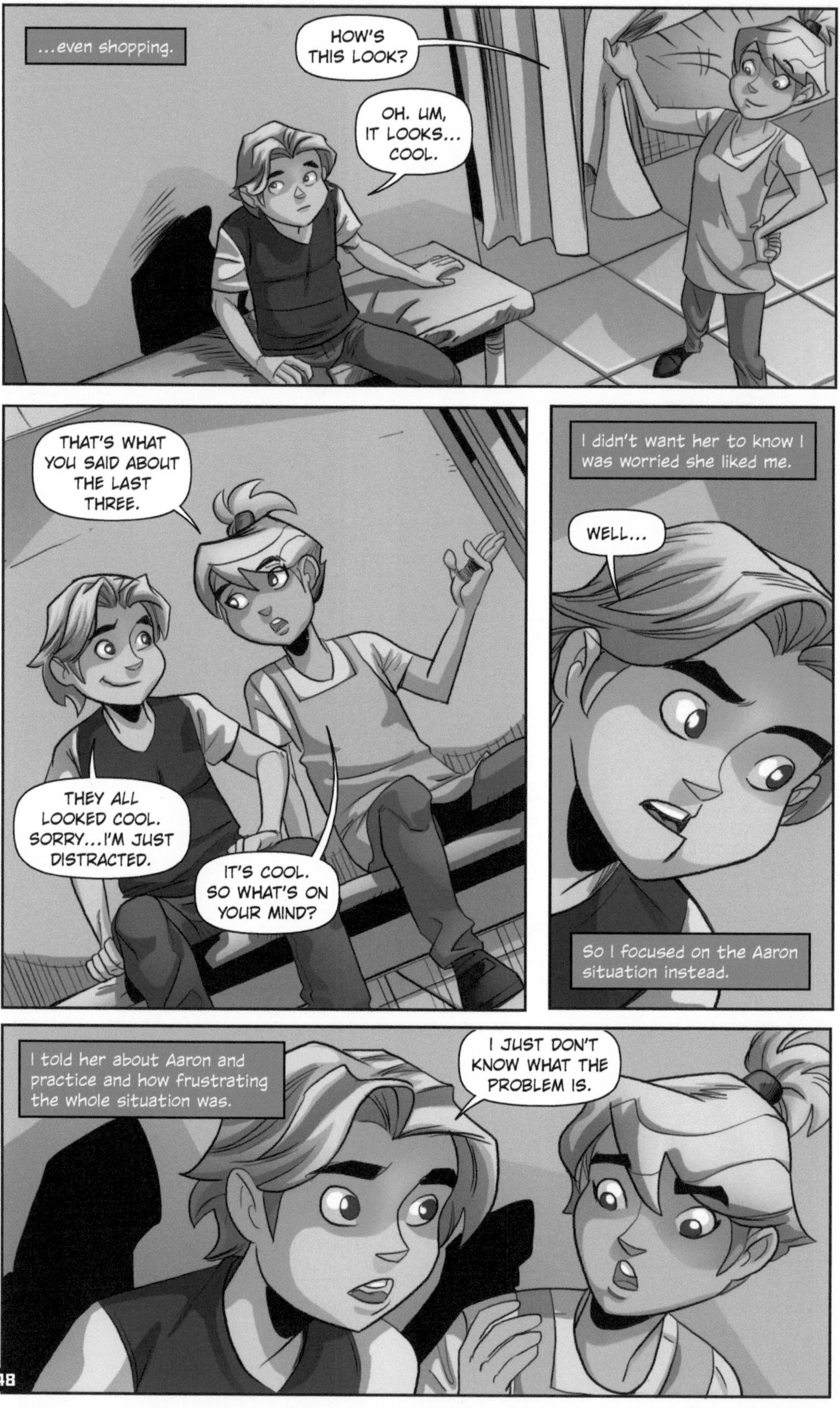
...even shopping.
HOW'S THIS LOOK?
OH. UM, IT LOOKS... COOL.
THAT'S WHAT YOU SAID ABOUT THE LAST THREE.
THEY ALL LOOKED COOL. SORRY...I'M JUST DISTRACTED.
IT'S COOL. SO WHAT'S ON YOUR MIND?
I didn't want her to know I was worried she liked me.
WELL...
So I focused on the Aaron situation instead.
I told her about Aaron and practice and how frustrating the whole situation was.
I JUST DON'T KNOW WHAT THE PROBLEM IS.

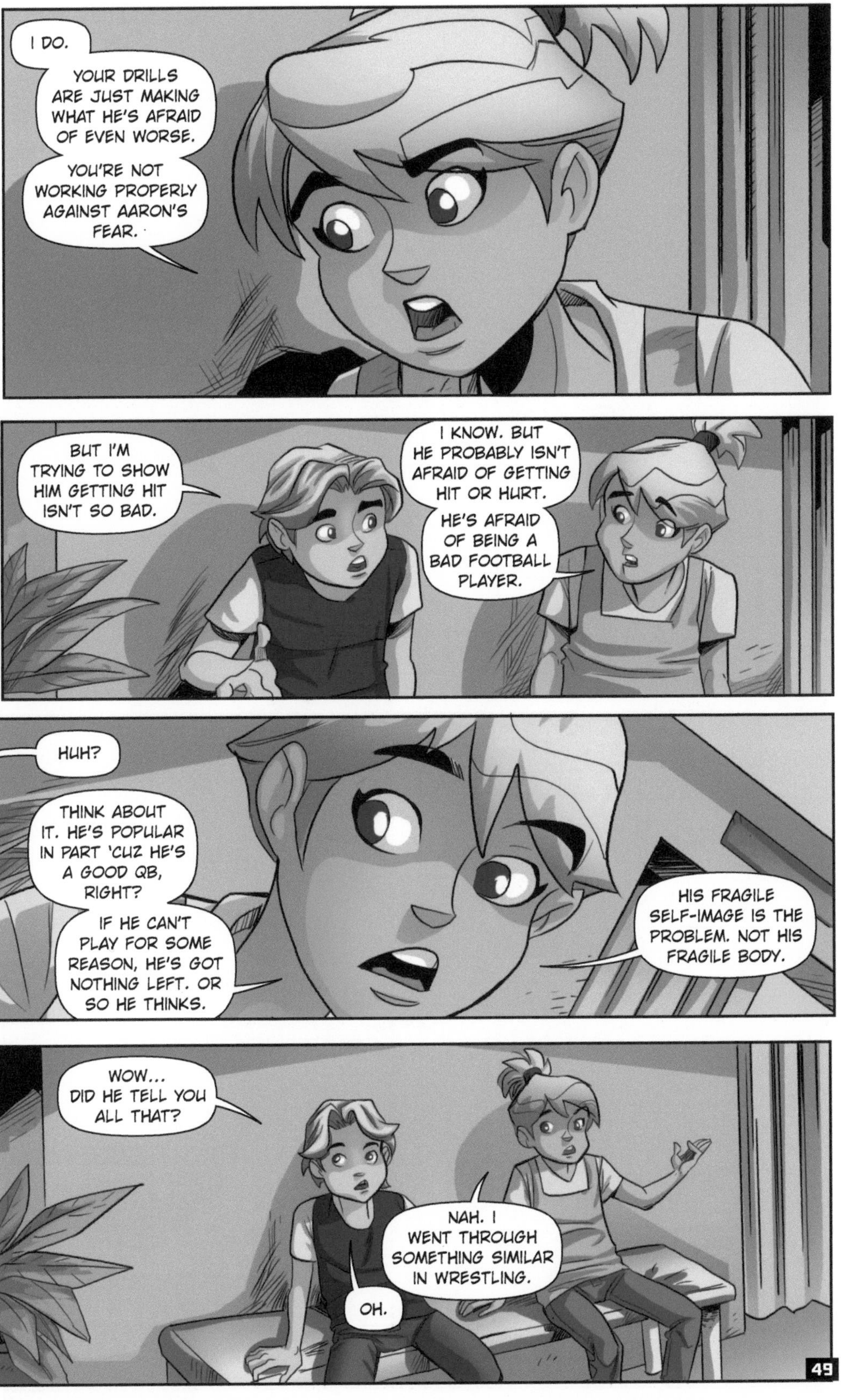
I DO.
YOUR DRILLS ARE JUST MAKING WHAT HE'S AFRAID OF EVEN WORSE.
YOU'RE NOT WORKING PROPERLY AGAINST AARON'S FEAR.
BUT I'M TRYING TO SHOW HIM GETTING HIT ISN'T SO BAD.
I KNOW. BUT HE PROBABLY ISN'T AFRAID OF GETTING HIT OR HURT.
HE'S AFRAID OF BEING A BAD FOOTBALL PLAYER.
HUH?
THINK ABOUT IT. HE'S POPULAR IN PART 'CUZ HE'S A GOOD QB, RIGHT?
IF HE CAN'T PLAY FOR SOME REASON, HE'S GOT NOTHING LEFT. OR SO HE THINKS.
HIS FRAGILE SELF-IMAGE IS THE PROBLEM. NOT HIS FRAGILE BODY.
WOW... DID HE TELL YOU ALL THAT?
NAH. I WENT THROUGH SOMETHING SIMILAR IN WRESTLING.
OH.

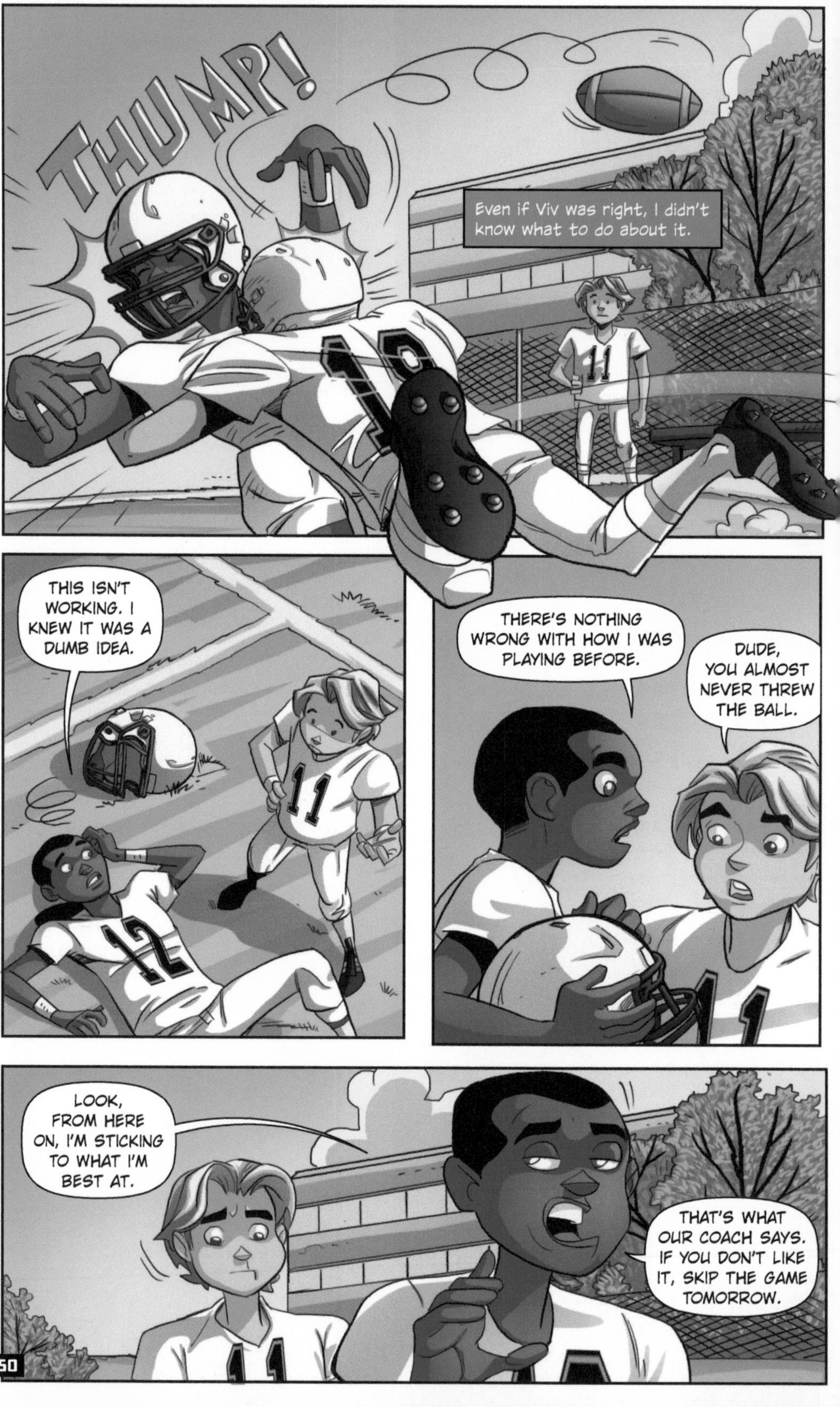
THUMP!
Even if Viv was right, I didn't know what to do about it.
THIS ISN'T WORKING. I KNEW IT WAS A DUMB IDEA.
THERE'S NOTHING WRONG WITH HOW I WAS PLAYING BEFORE.
DUDE, YOU ALMOST NEVER THREW THE BALL.
LOOK, FROM HERE ON, I'M STICKING TO WHAT I'M BEST AT.
THAT'S WHAT OUR COACH SAYS. IF YOU DON'T LIKE IT, SKIP THE GAME TOMORROW.

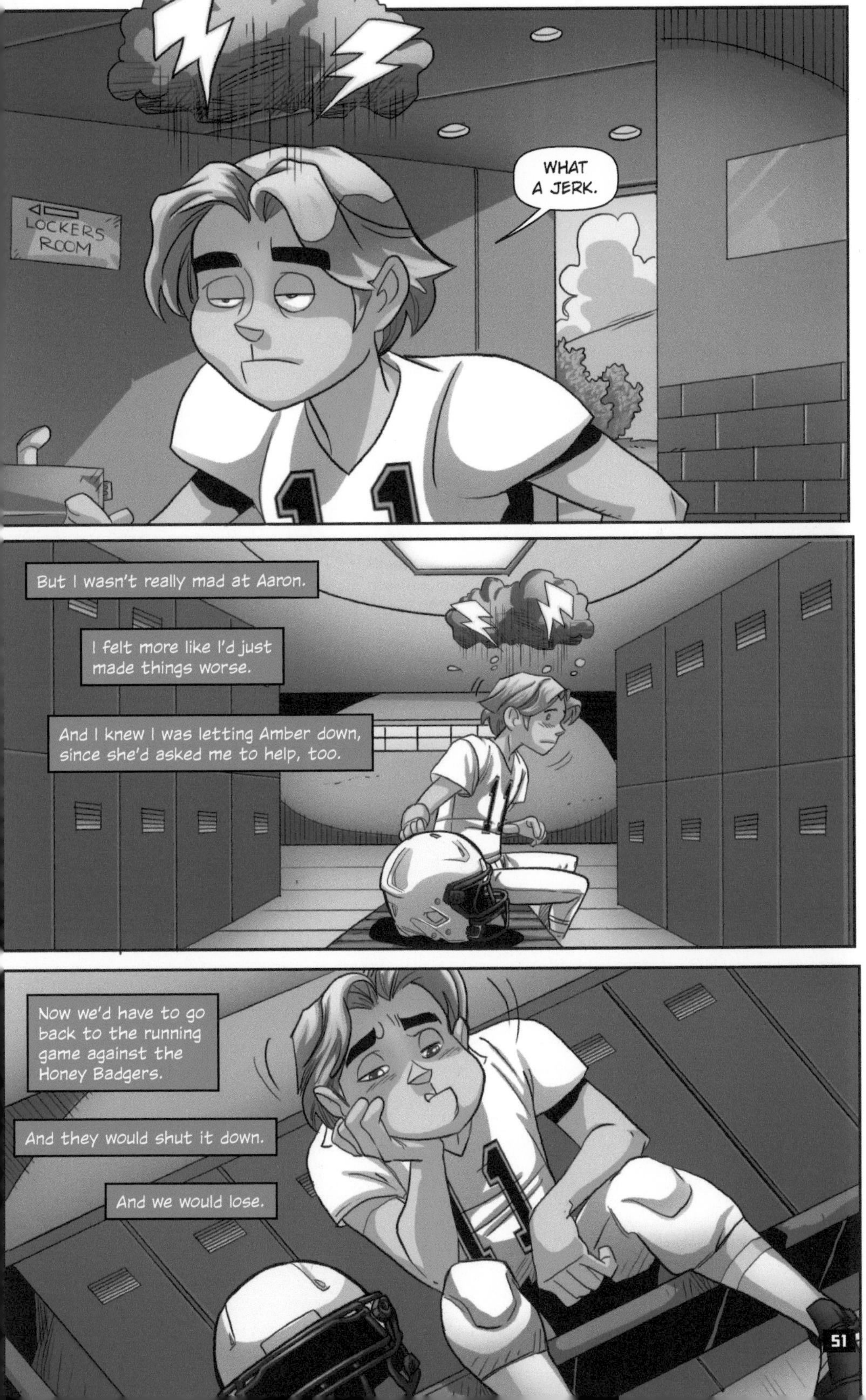
LOCKERS ROOM
WHAT A JERK.
But I wasn't really mad at Aaron.
I felt more like I'd just made things worse.
And I knew I was letting Amber down, since she'd asked me to help, too.
Now we'd have to go back to the running game against the Honey Badgers.
And they would shut it down.
And we would lose.

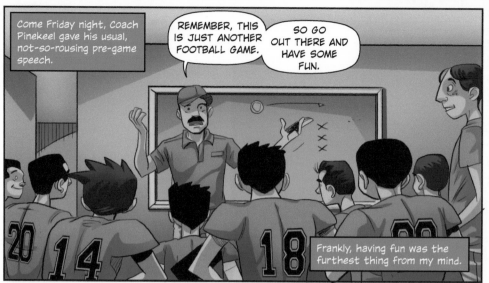

Come Friday night, Coach Pinekeel gave his usual, not-so-rousing pre-game speech.

REMEMBER, THIS IS JUST ANOTHER FOOTBALL GAME.

SO GO OUT THERE AND HAVE SOME FUN.

Frankly, having fun was the furthest thing from my mind.

FAILURE

I couldn't shake what felt like a cloud looming overhead.

And I wasn't alone. The team seemed affected, too.

At least the weather was nice.

Sigh...

The Honey Badgers returned our opening kickoff for a touchdown.

At least we didn't let them score again in the first quarter. Our defense was pretty tight.

But so was theirs.

We got a big interception and ran it back for a TD.

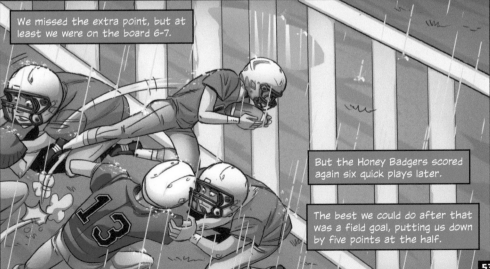

We missed the extra point, but at least we were on the board 6-7.

But the Honey Badgers scored again six quick plays later.

The best we could do after that was a field goal, putting us down by five points at the half.

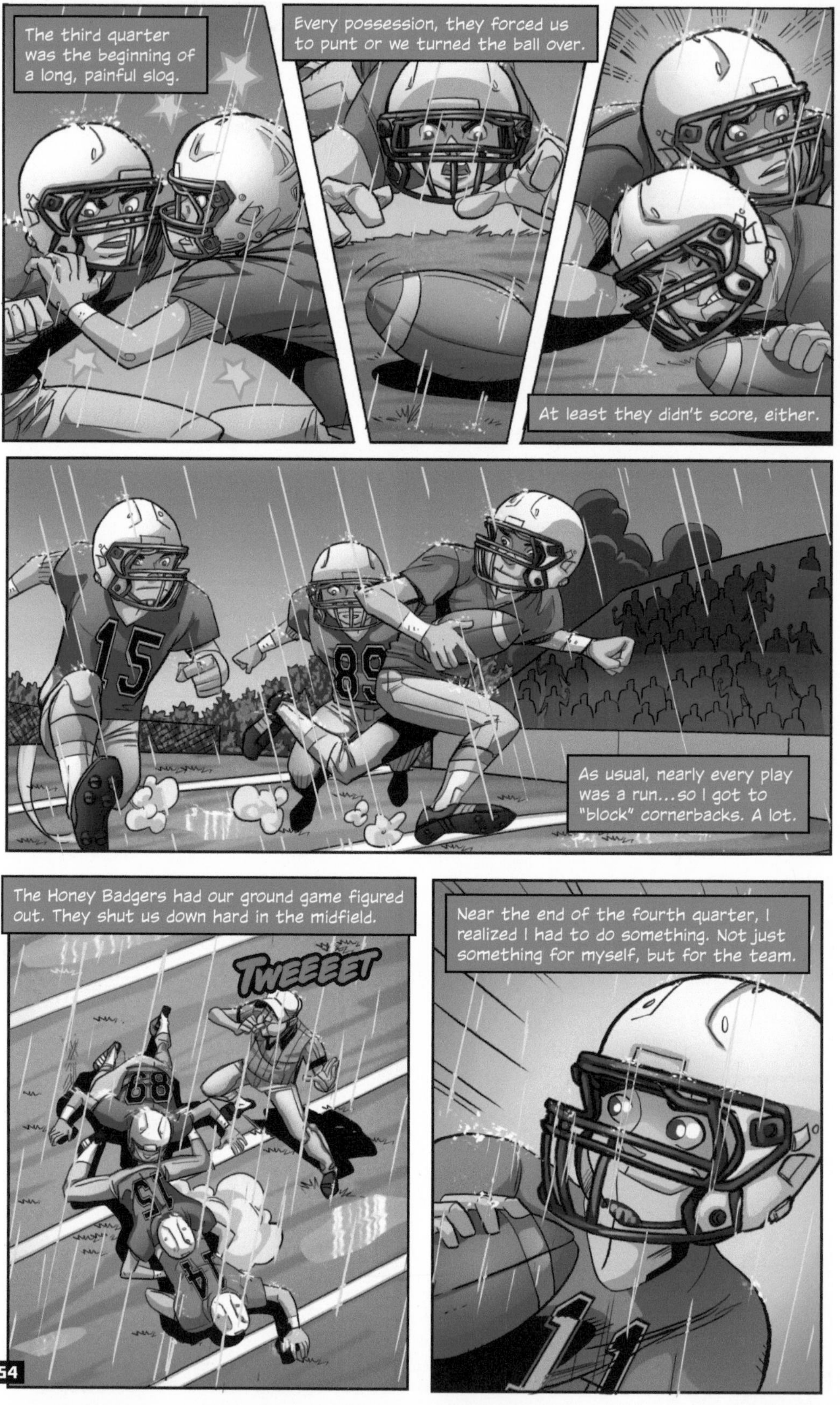
The third quarter was the beginning of a long, painful slog.
Every possession, they forced us to punt or we turned the ball over.
At least they didn't score, either.
15
89
As usual, nearly every play was a run...so I got to "block" cornerbacks. A lot.
The Honey Badgers had our ground game figured out. They shut us down hard in the midfield.
TWEEEET
Near the end of the fourth quarter, I realized I had to do something. Not just something for myself, but for the team.

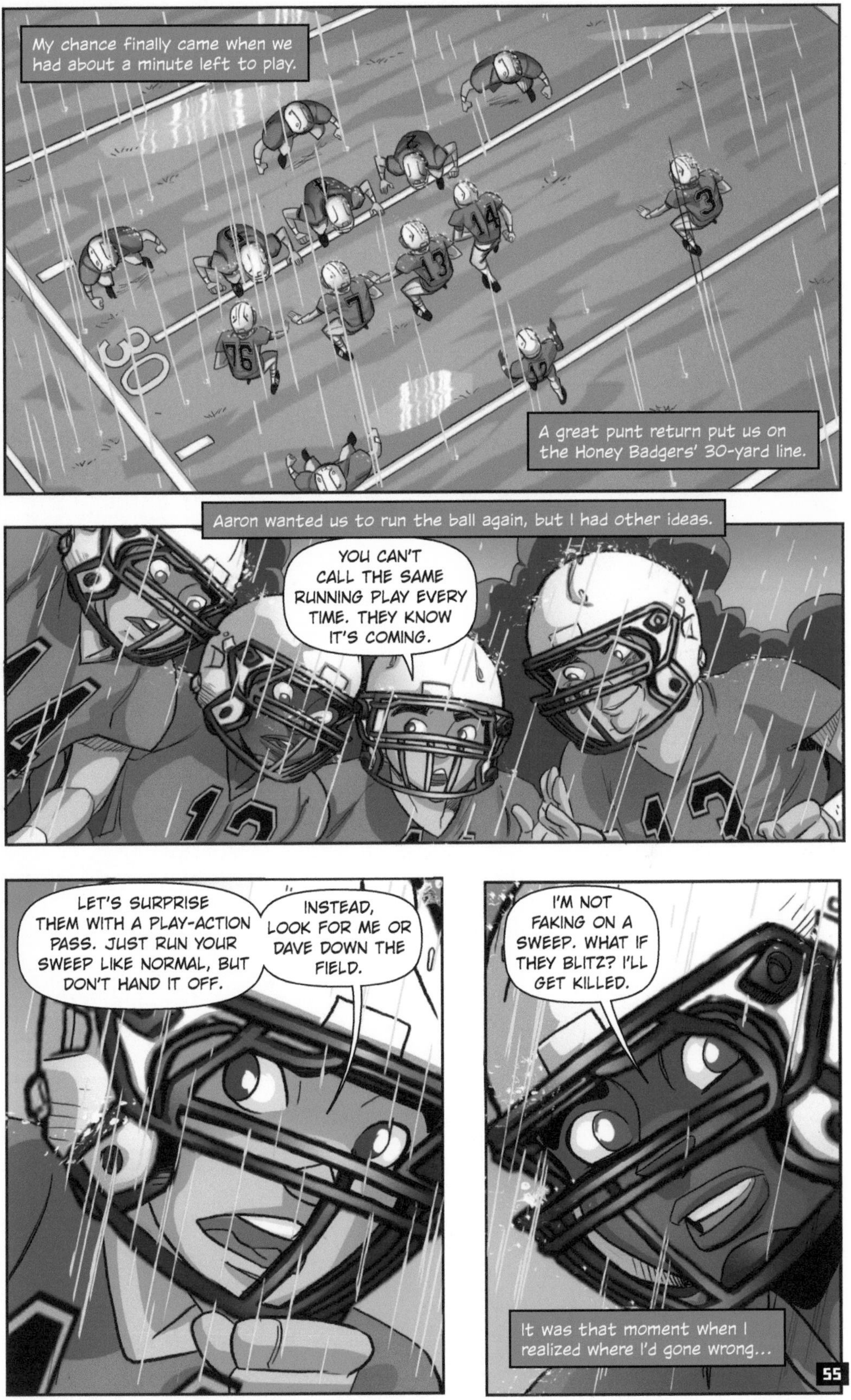

My chance finally came when we had about a minute left to play.
A great punt return put us on the Honey Badgers' 30-yard line.
30
Aaron wanted us to run the ball again, but I had other ideas.
YOU CAN'T CALL THE SAME RUNNING PLAY EVERY TIME. THEY KNOW IT'S COMING.
LET'S SURPRISE THEM WITH A PLAY-ACTION PASS. JUST RUN YOUR SWEEP LIKE NORMAL, BUT DON'T HAND IT OFF.
INSTEAD, LOOK FOR ME OR DAVE DOWN THE FIELD.
I'M NOT FAKING ON A SWEEP. WHAT IF THEY BLITZ? I'LL GET KILLED.
It was that moment when I realized where I'd gone wrong...

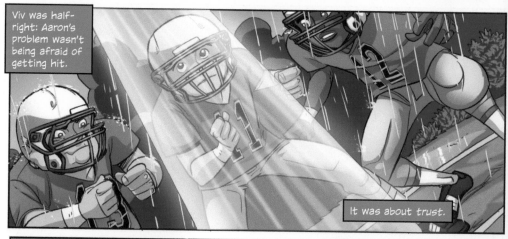

Viv was half-right: Aaron's problem wasn't being afraid of getting hit.

It was about trust.

The offensive line at his old school had let him down, and he'd gotten hurt.

Now he had no trust that our offensive line would protect him.

I knew what I had to do.

HEY MAN, I KNOW YOUR OLD LINEMEN LET YOU DOWN AND YOU GOT HURT.

BUT THESE GUYS WON'T LET THAT HAPPEN. TRUST THEM, THEY'LL PROTECT YOU.

NED, BACK ME UP HERE.

NOBODY'S GOING TO LAY A FINGER ON YOU WHILE I'M AROUND.

WE GOT YOUR BACK, BRO.

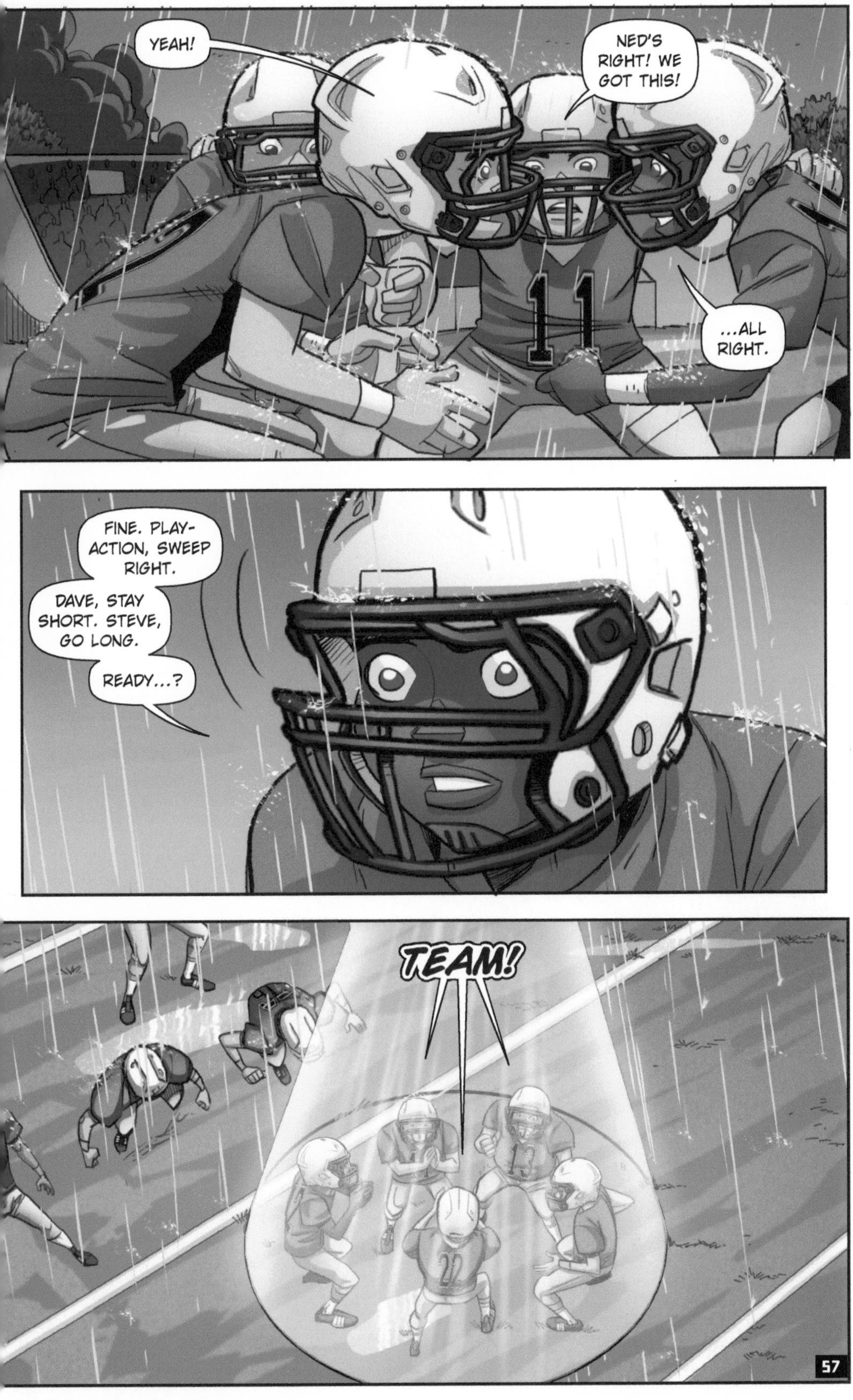
YEAH!
NED'S RIGHT! WE GOT THIS!
...ALL RIGHT.
FINE. PLAY-ACTION, SWEEP RIGHT.
DAVE, STAY SHORT. STEVE, GO LONG.
READY...?
TEAM!

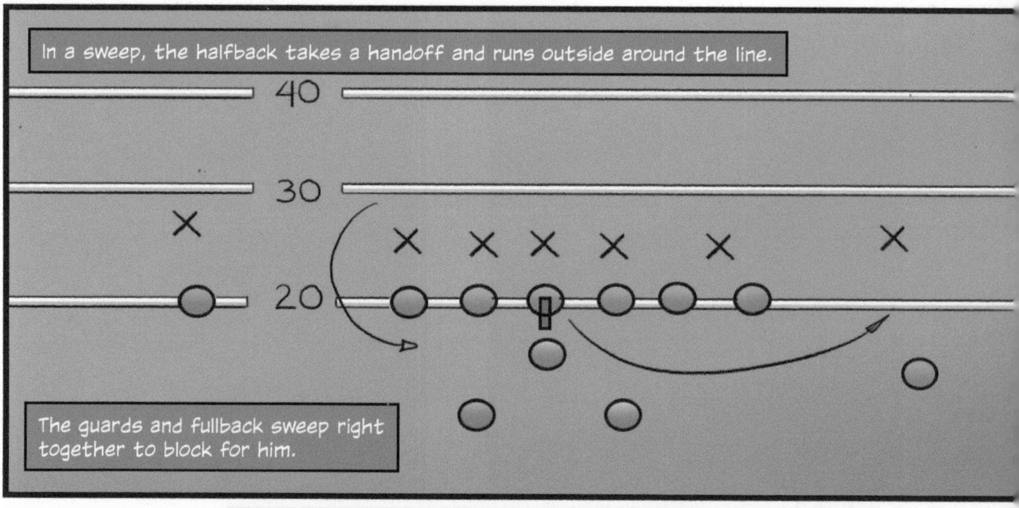
In a sweep, the halfback takes a handoff and runs outside around the line.
40
30
20
The guards and fullback sweep right together to block for him.

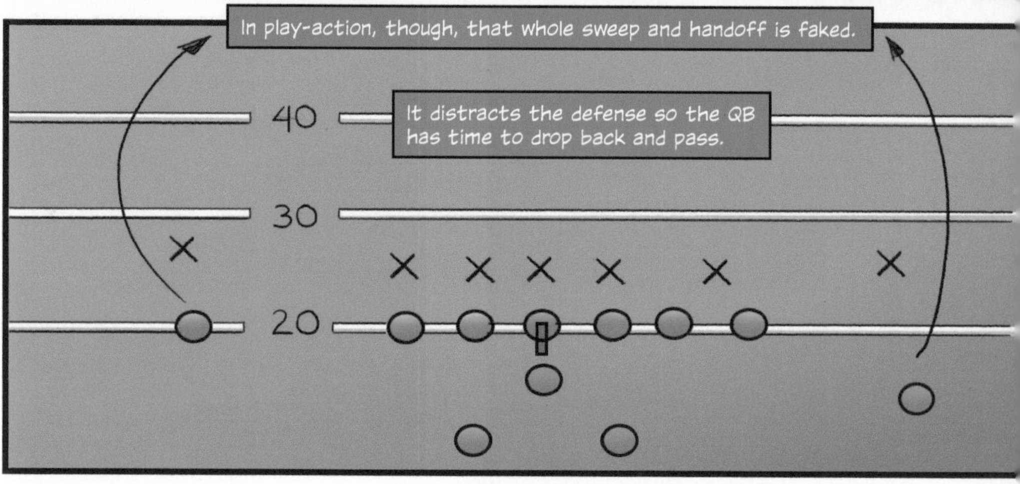
In play-action, though, that whole sweep and handoff is faked.
40
It distracts the defense so the QB has time to drop back and pass.
30
20

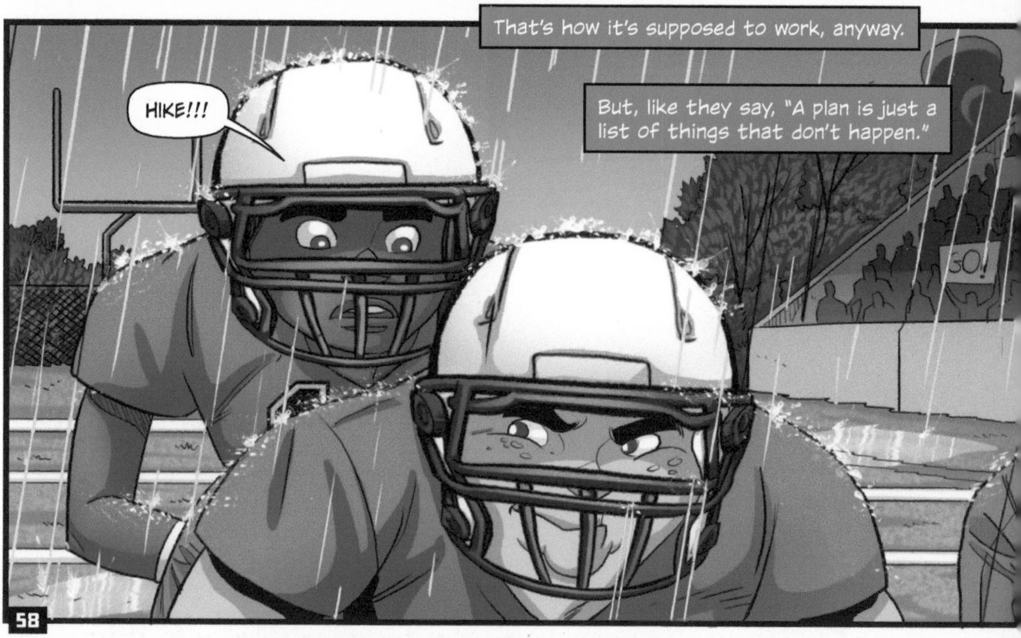
That's how it's supposed to work, anyway.
HIKE!!!
But, like they say, "A plan is just a list of things that don't happen."
GO!

Aaron forgot to fake the hand off.

I don't know why. Maybe he wanted to stay in control. Maybe it was just nerves.

Either way, the Honey Badgers knew that Aaron wasn't a passing threat.

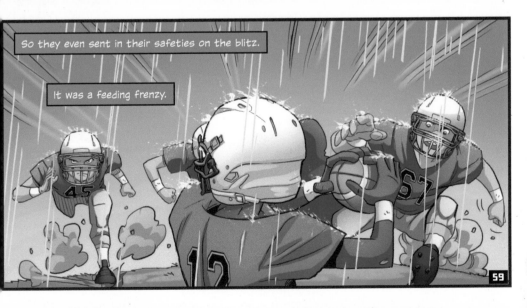

So they even sent in their safeties on the blitz.

It was a feeding frenzy.

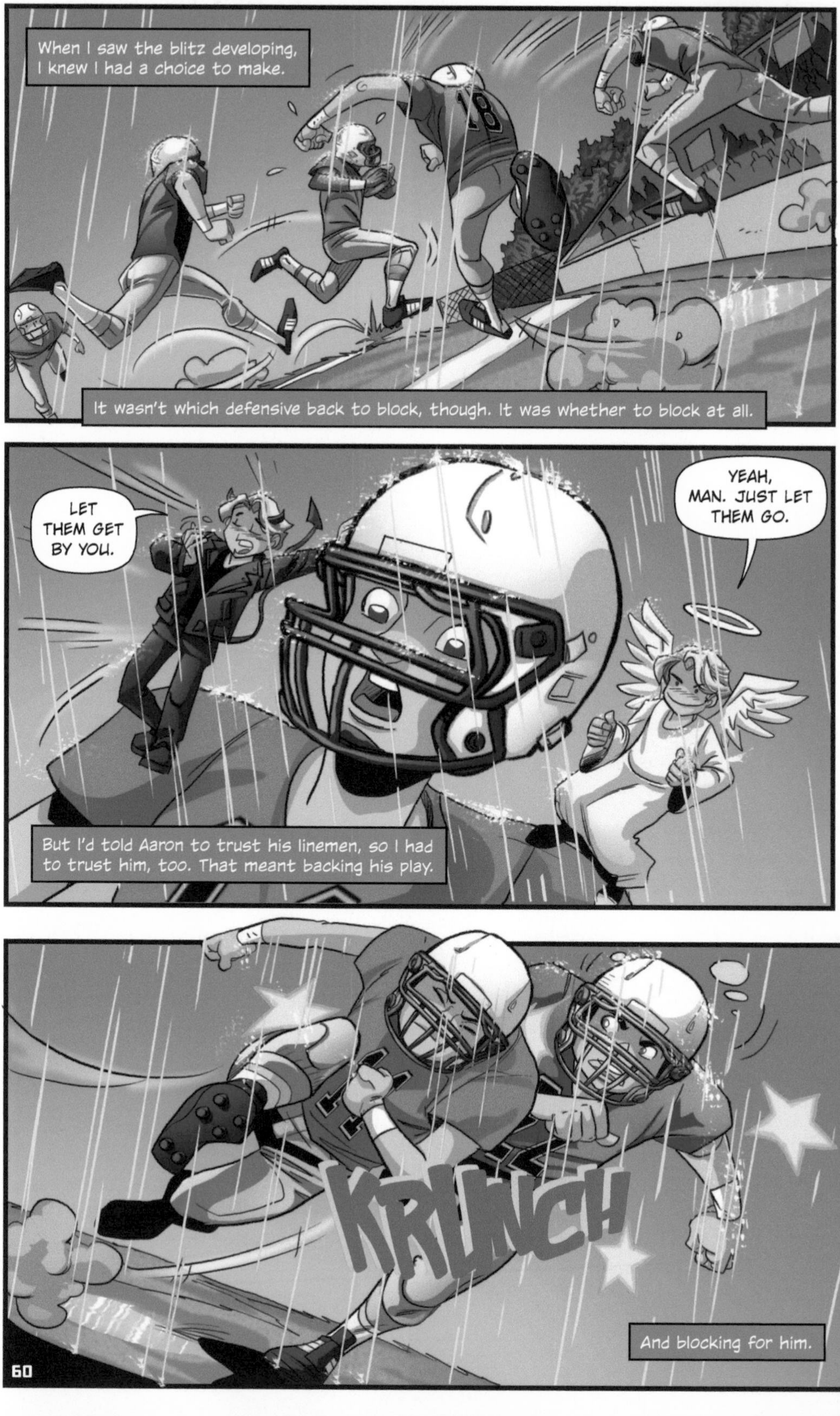
When I saw the blitz developing, I knew I had a choice to make.
It wasn't which defensive back to block, though. It was whether to block at all.
LET THEM GET BY YOU.
YEAH, MAN. JUST LET THEM GO.
But I'd told Aaron to trust his linemen, so I had to trust him, too. That meant backing his play.
KRUNCH
And blocking for him.

I watched as Aaron scrambled again. It looked like he was going to rush it himself.

Again.

But then Aaron surprised me.

NOW, NED!!!

I GOT YOU, BRO!

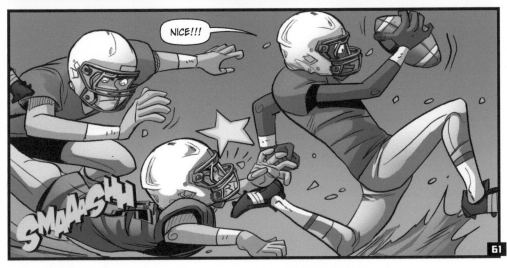

NICE!!!

SMAAASHH

WOOSH

That block gave Aaron all the time he needed to find me downfield.

Because of the blitz, I was wide open.

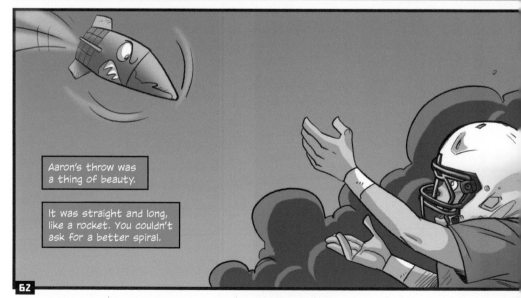

Aaron's throw was a thing of beauty.

It was straight and long, like a rocket. You couldn't ask for a better spiral.

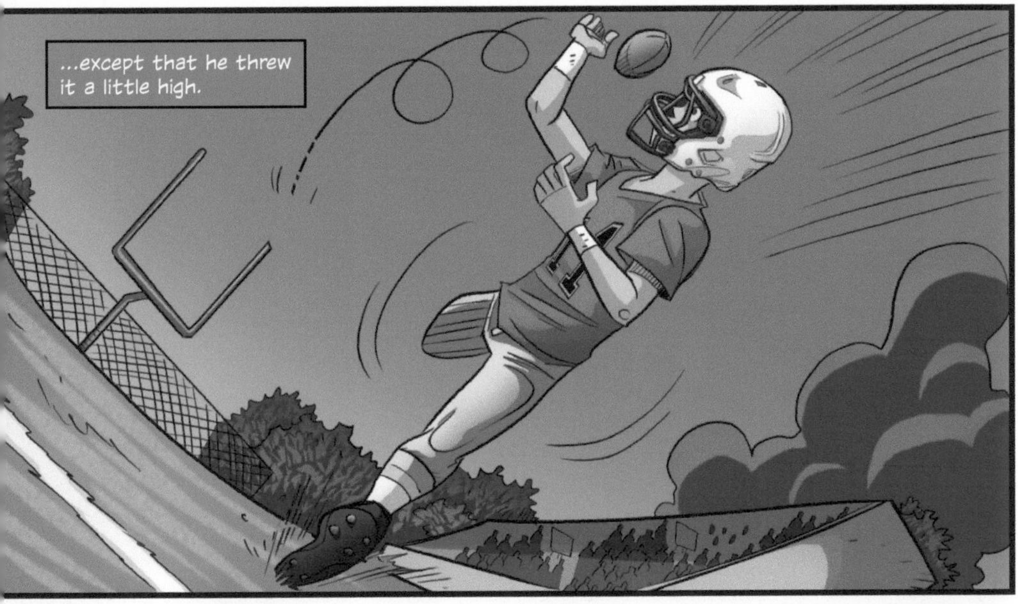
...except that he threw it a little high.
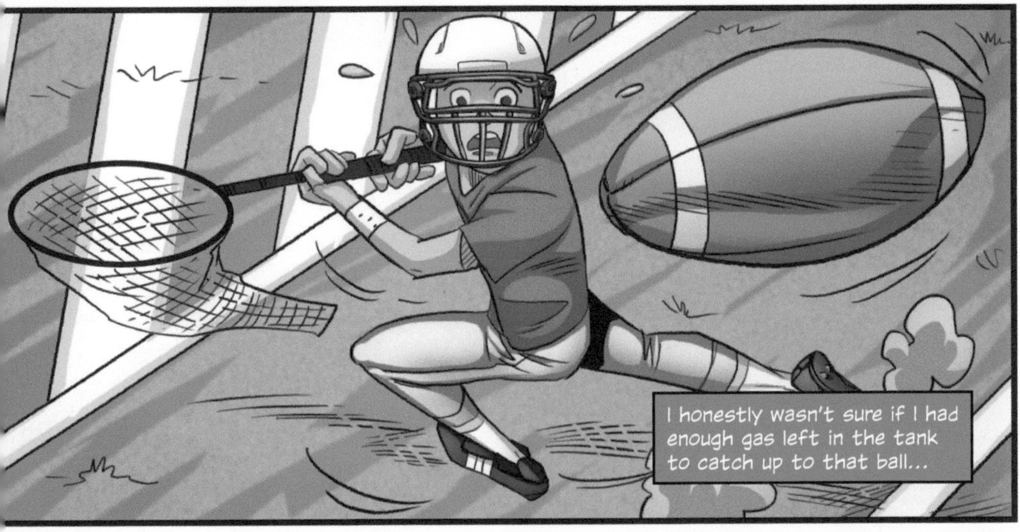
I honestly wasn't sure if I had enough gas left in the tank to catch up to that ball...
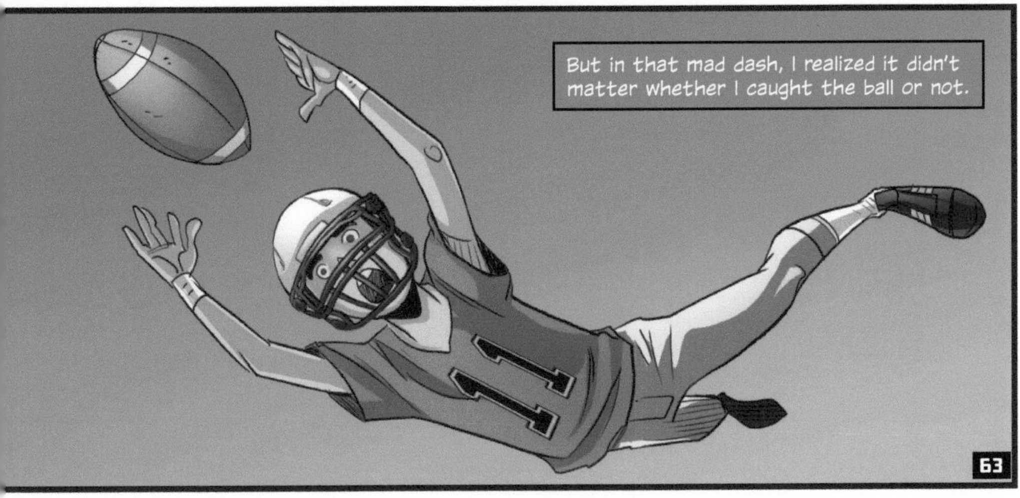
But in that mad dash, I realized it didn't matter whether I caught the ball or not.

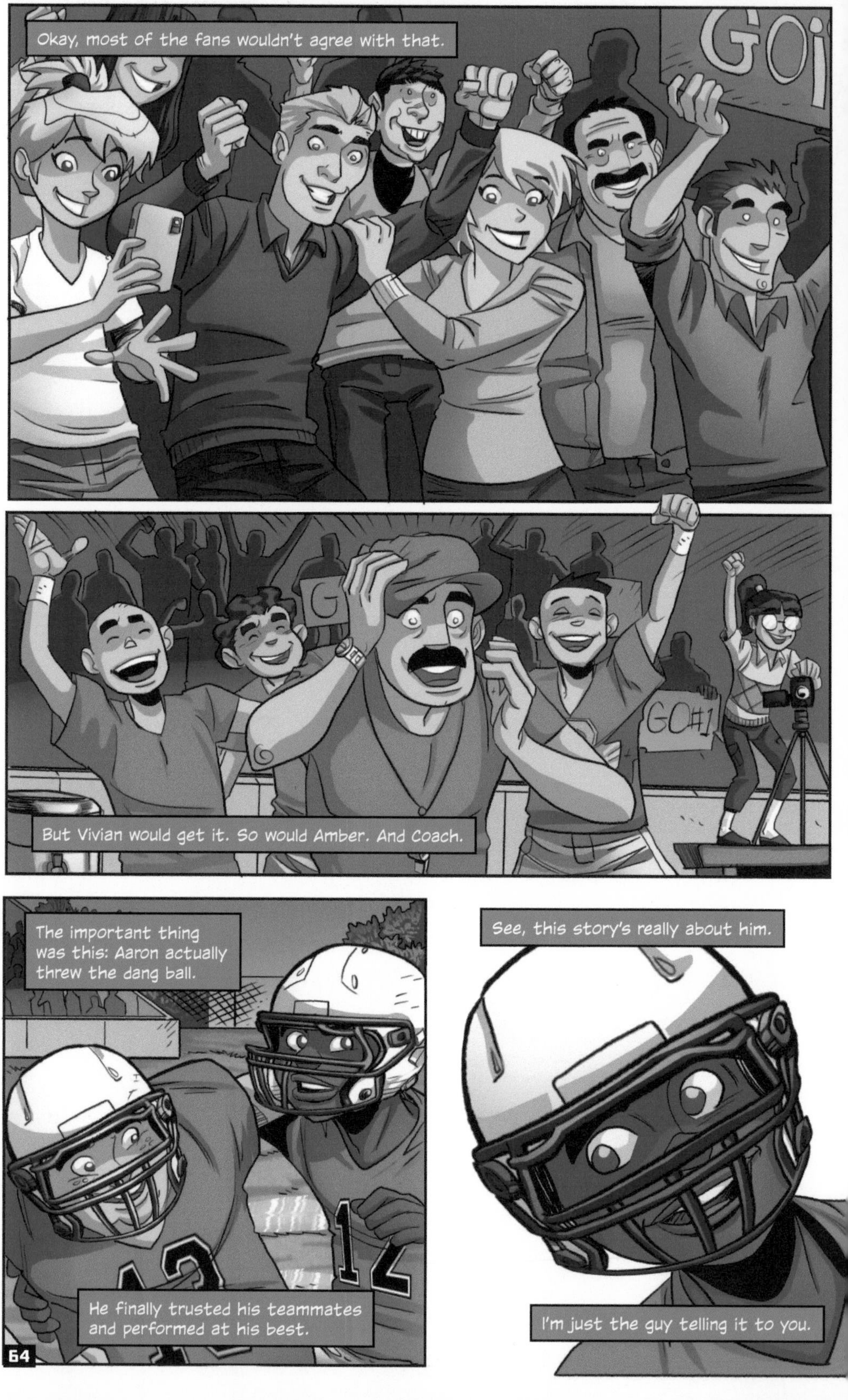
Okay, most of the fans wouldn't agree with that.
GO!
GO
GO#1
But Vivian would get it. So would Amber. And Coach.
The important thing was this: Aaron actually threw the dang ball.
He finally trusted his teammates and performed at his best.
See, this story's really about him.
I'm just the guy telling it to you.

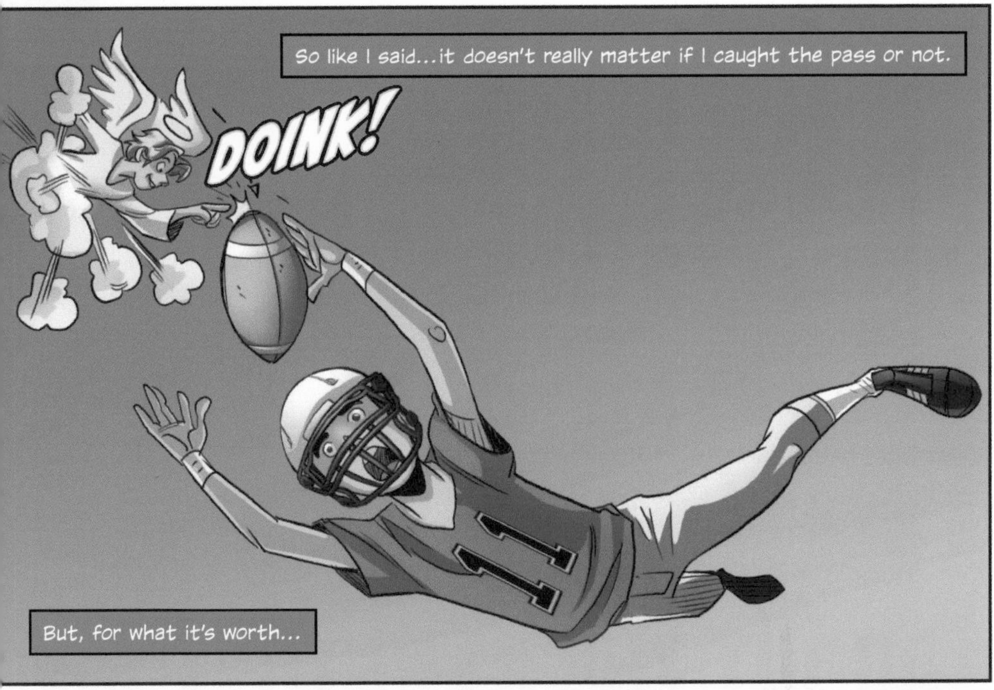
So like I said...it doesn't really matter if I caught the pass or not.
DOINK!
But, for what it's worth...

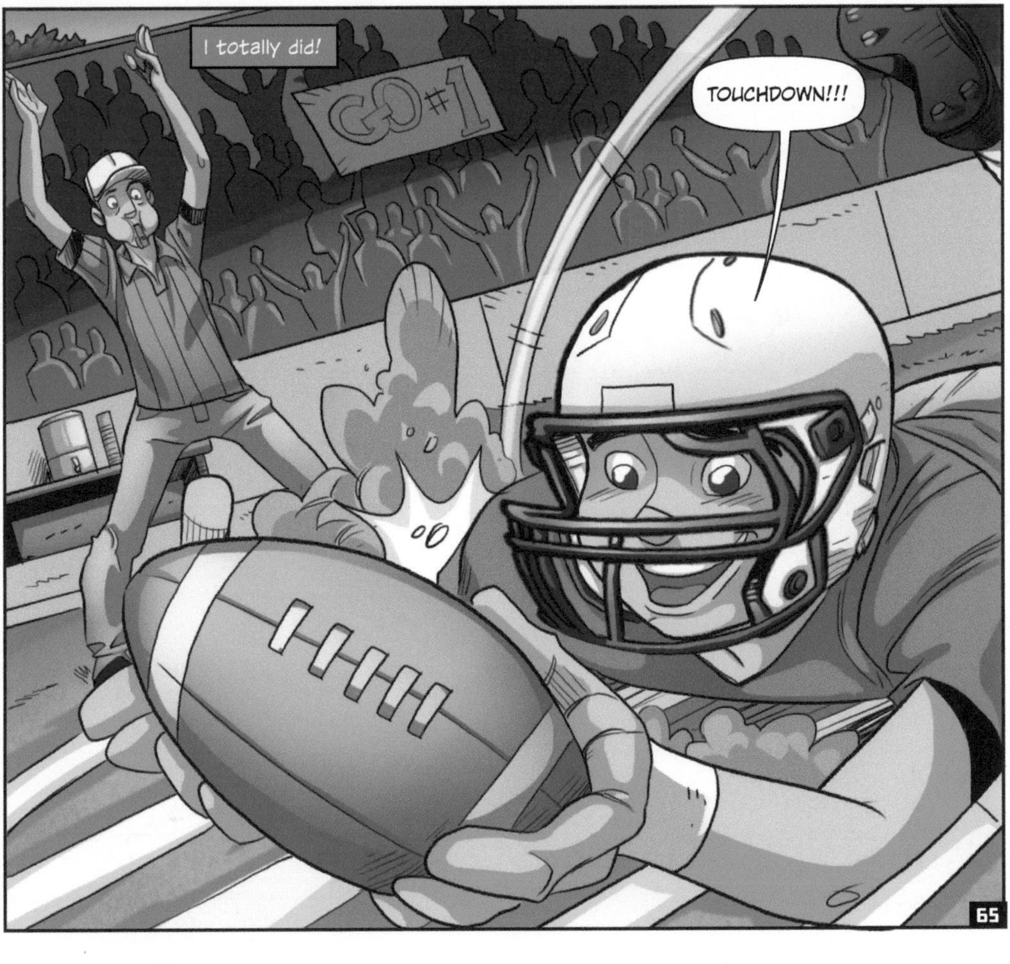
I totally did!
GO #1
TOUCHDOWN!!!

ABOUT THE AUTHOR

CARL BOWEN is a father, husband, and writer living in Lawrenceville, Georgia. He has published a handful of novels, short stories, and comics. For Stone Arch Books and Capstone, Carl has retold *20,000 Leagues Under the Sea* (by Jules Verne), *The Strange Case of Dr. Jekyll and Mr. Hyde* (by Robert Louis Stevenson), *The Jungle Book* (by Rudyard Kipling), "Aladdin, and His Wonderful Lamp" (from *A Thousand and One Nights*), *Julius Caesar* (by William Shakespeare), and *The Murders in the Rue Morgue* (by Edgar Allan Poe). Carl's novel, *Shadow Squadron: Elite Infantry*, earned a starred review from Kirkus Book Reviews.

ABOUT THE ILLUSTRATOR

Working out of Mexico City, passionate comic book fan and artist **EDUARDO GARCIA** has lent his talented illustration abilities to such varied projects as the Spider-Man Family, Flash Gordon, and Speed Racer. He's currently working on a series of illustrations for an educational publisher while his wife and children look over his shoulder!

ABOUT THE LETTERER

JAYMES REED has operated the company Digital-CAPS: Comic Book Lettering since 2003. He has done lettering for many publishers, most notably and recently Avatar Press. He's also the only letterer working with Inception Strategies, an Aboriginal-Australian publisher that develops social comics with public service messages for the Australian government. Jaymes also a 2012 & 2013 Shel Dorf Award Nominee.

GLOSSARY

ARROGANT (AIR-uh-guhnt)—overly proud of oneself or one's own opinions

CONDITIONING (kuhn-DISH-uh-ning)—exercise for sports used to get athletes in better physical shape

EVIDENCE (EV-i-duhnss)—material or statements that help prove something

FRAGILE (FRAJ-uhl)—easily broken or destroyed

INTEGRITY (in-TEG-ri-tee)—if you have integrity, you are honest and sincere

INTERVENTION (in-ter-VEN-shuhn)—if you hold an intervention for someone, you gather their family and friends and confront them about a difficult subject

JUDGMENT (JUDGE-ment)—if you have good judgment, your perspective is sound and you make good decisions

PANIC (PAN-ik)—if you panic, you let sudden fear overwhelm you

PLAY-ACTION (PLAY AK-shuhn)—a play in football where the quarterback fakes a handoff to a running back, then drops back to pass

PRACTICALLY (PRAK-tik-lee)—almost or nearly

LOOPY (LOO-pee)—moving in a semi-circular manner. A loopy pass lacks the tight spiral of a good pass.

SUPPRESS (suh-PRESS)—to keep from being known by the use of authority or force

VARIATIONS (vayr-ee-AY-shuhnz)—changes in form, position, or condition

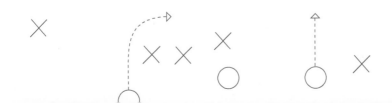

VISUAL QUESTIONS

1. What do the little imaginary birds around Steve's head mean? Why did the comic book's creators choose to put them there?

2. Why do the borders of this panel look wavy, and why is the color muted? Reread page 13 for clues.

3. Why does this zombie's head pass over the panel's top border? Can you think of a reason why an illustrator would choose to do this?

4. What's going on with the steam rising from Steve's neck in this panel? What do you think it means?

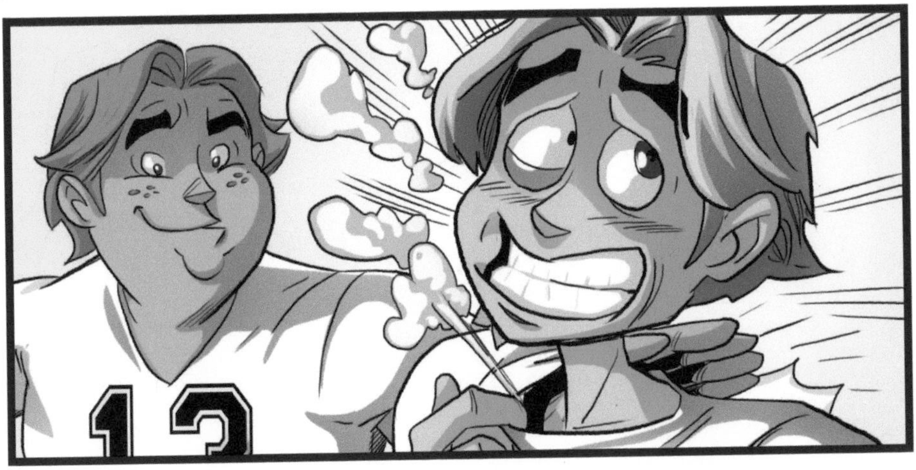

5. Why is there a spotlight shining down on Steve here? What do you think it means in terms of the plot or story?

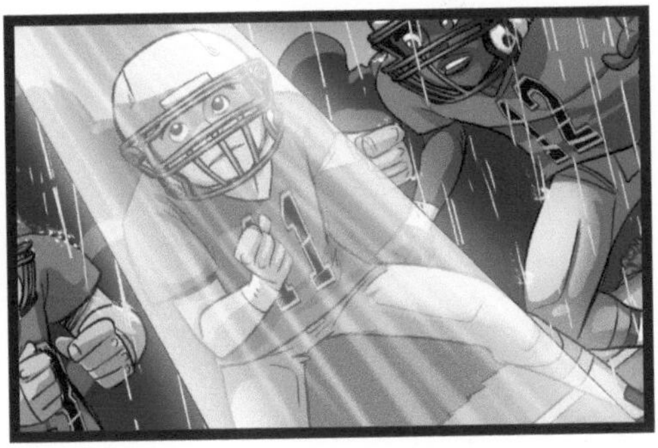

6. In the panel below, we see lightning bolts, a dashed line, and a bomb. How do these elements make you feel about what's going on in the panel?

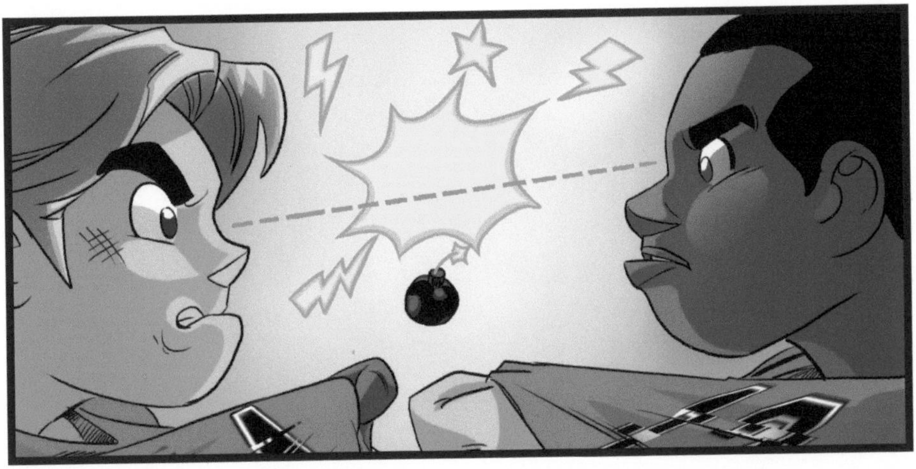

READ THEM ALL!

Sports Illustrated KIDS
GRAPHIC NOVELS
8-BIT BASEBALL
TERRELL · FERRARA

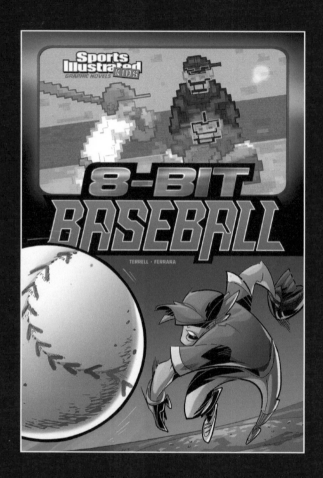

8–BIT BASEBALL

Jared Richards is undefeated in baseball games—video games, anyway. But when he loses a bet to his best friend, Jared is forced to get off the couch and step onto the field for his school's baseball team tryouts. Despite the fact that he's never even held a baseball before, Jared ends up being pretty impressive as a pitcher—until the line between video games and reality begins to blur. Can Jared sort out the glitch in his brain before he blows the big game?

Sports Illustrated KIDS
SPOTLIGHT SOCCER
SANCHEZ • WARYANTO

SPOTLIGHT SOCCER

More than anything else, Franco dreams of going pro some day. After all, his soccer coaches say he's the best kind of player—more giving than greedy, preferring to rack up the assists instead of scoring goals. And that method works just fine until Franco has to change schools. On his new team, Franco's pass-first approach to soccer just isn't working. To make matters worse, the team is filled with ball-hogs, and their coach doesn't seem to care about anything. Franco refuses to let his dream of going pro die, but the new team is pretty much a living nightmare.

Sports Illustrated KIDS
BEASTLY BASKETBALL
JOHNSON • GARCIA

BEASTLY BASKETBALL

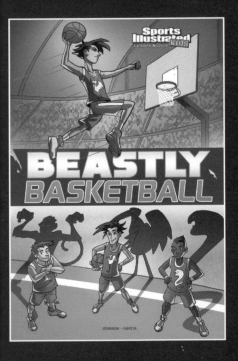

Joe knows kung fu. In fact, he loves it more than anything. Every single evening, Joe walks to his neighborhood kung fu studio to practice for hours on end . . . until the day he arrives to find his studio has closed—permanently. So, Joe decides to pursue his second-favorite activity—basketball. He joins his school's team only to find that the players are disorganized, timid, and lacking in discipline! So, Joe uses his experience in martial arts to bring out the best—or beast!—in his teammates! Will their newfound skills lead to flawless victory, or will they continue to get beaten to the punch?

PLAYBOOK

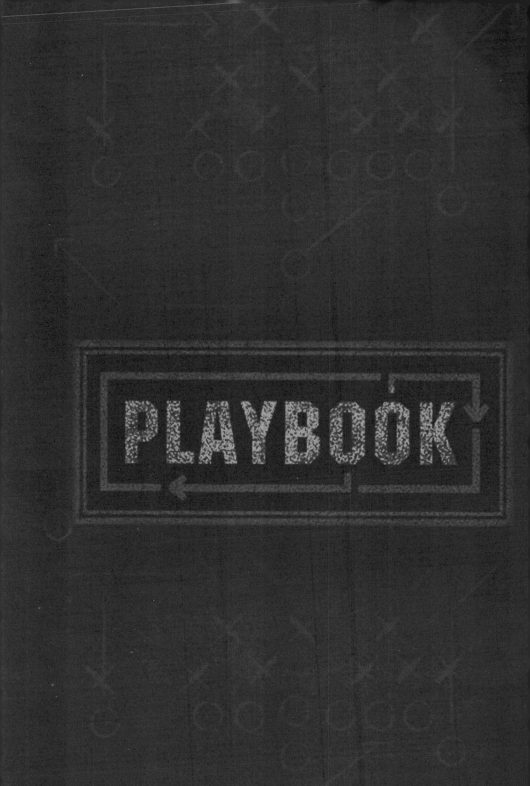